William

A novel by Larry Timbs Jr.
& Michael Manuel

Based on a screenplay by
Michael Manuel

ISBN: 978-1-959700-39-5

Hoot Books Publishing
Victoria Fletcher
851 French Moore Blvd.
Abingdon, VA 24210

Acknowledgments from Larry Timbs Jr.

Thank you to my good friend Michael Manuel for creating the screenplay several years ago for William.

Writing a novel is not an easy task. But I benefited greatly from having Michael's screenplay to guide me.

Michael has quite an imagination as well as a knack for capturing the colorful and sometimes unpredictable nuances of human behavior.

The novel *William* hopefully is a testament to his considerable literary skills.

As for yours truly, I began writing *William* soon after I suffered a double broken ankle. It has been a long recovery process, and one, ironically enough, during which I spent many hours writing about a young boy's "special feet."

Maybe a curious case of life imitating art or vice versa.

Thank you to my close friend and mentor (and former boss in the newspaper industry) Max Heath who passed away a few years ago in Kentucky. Max thought the highest calling in the world was to be a journalist.

While *William* isn't journalism, I'd like to think Max would appreciate its simplicity, clarity, and attention to detail.

Acknowledgments from Michael Manuel

A heartfelt thanks to my friend and co-author Larry C. Timbs Jr. for saving my story, *William.*

I wrote *William* as a screenplay in hopes of having a movie made. Then, after a few failed attempts, it slept in the documents of my computer for several years, until Larry asked to read it again. Seeing its potential, Larry spent many months adapting *William* into a manuscript for a book. Then together we worked the next few months fine tuning the story. I will always be grateful to Larry for having the foresight to adapt *William* into this book.

Thanks to my daughter Leigh Manuel who has always supported my writing and to all my family and extended family members who have encouraged my writing over the years.

Thank you to my sister-in-law, Betty Manuel, for the editing of my screenplay of *William* and for her encouragement of my writing over the years.

Thank you to my lovely wife Joyce for again putting up with my days and nights spent in the office pounding away on the computer. I hope someday you will be rewarded for your patience. Love you.

Thank you to my grandson, Taylor Kyte, for taking the photos of the Butler bridge for the cover of the book.

Contents

CHAPTER 1

Nagging Questions

My name is William Anderson and I'm unlike anyone else in the world.

In fact, I'm so different that for most of my childhood, I could reveal my secret to absolutely no one.

That was my solemn promise to my dad, Ed Anderson, of Laketon, Tennessee.

Because he warned me that folks in these rugged East Tennessee mountains, where I was raised, wouldn't understand.

They just wouldn't be able to handle what I was or why the Good Lord had seen fit to make me so different.

Never mind that many of 'em attended church every Sunday.

And that these so-called God-fearing Christians professed abiding love to others.

Not that they were in any way hypocritical, but Dad said people, at their core, expected me to be just like everyone else.

They wanted me NOT to be different, and they didn't like things or folks that confused them.

"And son, you would rock their world," Dad reminded me over and over.

"It's best just to keep our secret between you and me and Doc Benson. We all do that, and you'll be just fine."

But that was a lot to ask a little kid, and I kept finding myself, more and more in my growing up years, wondering why God had made me the way he did.

"Son, I don't have an answer for you," he always said. But I'm sure he had a good reason."

Then he'd wrap me in his arms, hold me closely, and tell me again and again that he loved me. It was a lot for any little kid to try to understand.

Even though in some ways I was blessed to be born into a good home in a picture-perfect close-knit community.

Not far from Johnson City, Laketon was surrounded by some of the most beautiful mountains, roaring rivers, and lush forests in America.

"But why, Dad? Why did I have to be born this way?"

"Why couldn't I just be like my friend Raymond or Matt or Jim? I didn't do nothin' wrong, did I? You think God was tryin' to tell me somethin'?"

My dad, a slender man with a high furrowed forehead, sky blue eyes, broad shoulders, and close-cropped hair he combed straight back, never had a good answer for me.

Instead, he just told me to trust him and keep silent about how I was different.

And he made me promise him—again and again—never to break that trust.

CHAPTER 2

Twelve Years Earlier

It had all started on the storm-ravaged night on June 23rd of 1968, the night I was born.

Dad had lost his forever best friend, soulmate, and lover—his wife Daisy—a few years earlier.

So, he was used to dealing with sad, life-changing situations on his own.

Not that he had planned it that way because he and Daisy had been sweethearts all through high school. Wherever you saw Ed Anderson in those early years, you'd see Daisy. She had been blessed with sparkling blue eyes, long blond hair, and a shapely, fetching body that caught many a man's attention.

Ed and Daisy, from the moment they laid eyes on one another, had been inseparable. Almost every night had been a date night—with trips to the movies, the Dairy Queen, or just cruising the town in Ed's 1957 Chevy. And within a few months, as Daisy readied herself to enter college, the couple dreamed of getting married, buying a small plot of land, farming, and building a life together.

Their wedding, far as they were concerned, couldn't have happened soon enough. And it had been a beautiful occasion, with church bells clanging melodiously, groomsmen and bridesmaids dressed in matching outfits, countless well-wishers hugging both Daisy and Ed, and everyone sending them off in a state of pure happiness to their honeymoon in Gatlinburg.

"What a nice, sweet couple!" one of the elderly women at the wedding had remarked. "They are just perfect for one another."

But soon thereafter, in only the second year of their marriage, Daisy came down with pancreatic cancer. She fought hard, and Ed even took her to Vanderbilt to the best cancer specialist in Tennessee, but it was to no avail.

Her diseased body withered, and in the final days of her life, Daisy dropped to a mere 75 pounds.

"Don't worry about me," she would constantly reassure her grief-stricken husband Ed, who never left her bedside. "God's got this."

Then the couple would clasp their hands and whisper a fervent prayer that Daisy would somehow survive.

But her sweat-drenched, weakened, yellowed body only got weaker. And within a few months of being told she had the fatal disease, it was over.

Ed had been devastated. Because it was never supposed to have ended like this.

Instead of years together as man and wife and having children and experiencing all the joy and love that they were bound to have together, Ed now had to decide what to do with his life.

Months of counseling, his steadfast faith in the Almighty, and the tender kindness of good friends and neighbors helped him get through the crisis.

Still, however, he would never get over losing the love of his life.

*****

And so, it was late one unforgettable, storm-ravaged night that his son William came into this world.

Ed had been lying fully awake in his bed.

He hadn't been able to sleep because of the pounding rain and hen egg sized hail that slammed against the windows of his little white farmhouse. Even more unsettling was the 100 mile per hour wind and flashing, crackling lightning.

Ed feared the worst. Tornadoes were few and far between in these mountains, but they weren't unheard of. And he couldn't recall a storm that had seemed so severe.

Wanting to check on his long eared Nubian nanny goat that was expecting to give birth at any time now, Ed quickly put on a heavy slicker, patted his beloved slumbering dog Denny, a 70-pound yellow lab, on the head and started out the door.

"Come on boy," he said. "Somethin' tells me we better take a quick walk out ta' the barn."

But Denny wasn't cooperating. Instead, the big loveable slobberknocker swished his tail, cast his sad eyes toward his master, and lay back down.

Ed coaxed the dog with a piece of jerky and that did the trick. Denny, his ears raring back and his mouth wide open, stood up and took the bait, eagerly chomping down on the beefy treat.

"Okay, boy, now let's head out to the barn," Ed said.

A gust of ferocious wind and hail pressed hard against his house, threatening to blow it down, as man and dog made their way outside.

The howling wind, pounding rain and hail, and lightning, which crisscrossed the sky and seemed more threatening by the second, made their otherwise short trek to the barn seem dangerous.

He looked toward the barn and in the flashing lightning he could see barn doors swinging back and forth. And as he got closer, he heard an unusual sound—almost like a baby crying.

Small limbs and debris blew past Ed and his dog as they leaned into the wind, and, step by step, struggled onward.

Suddenly, Ed heard that mysterious sound again. It had a haunting strangeness to it that was hard to pin down.

If it wasn't from the storm, then what the heck could it be? he wondered.

"Come on, boy," Ed beckoned his dog, close by his side. "We're almost there."

Arriving at the barn, Ed found that the doors had come unlatched and were banging against the main structure. So, he quickly closed the heavy doors and latched them shut from the inside.

The rain and hail on the barn's tin roof was deafening, and Ed could see lightning flashes through cracks in the old barn's dilapidated walls.

The smell of hay and animal manure filled his senses as Ed, clicking on his flashlight, began going from stall to stall and checking on his livestock.

In the first stall was a large Nubian billy goat lying on the straw-covered floor and chewing on his cud. Two small kids were curled up nearby.

Ed's dog Denny, his tail wagging, took a few sniffs and licked one of the kids on the face. The baby goat didn't move and even seemed to like the attention.

"Come on, Denny. Let's check on Marshmallow. She's the one expecting."

The dog made eye contact with Ed, seeming to understand what he just said, and trotted obediently beside him.

Guided by the beam of the flashlight, they walked to another stall.

But then the flashlight started flickering in the darkness. Ed, coaxing the light to stay on, hit it on the bottom end, and presto, the light shined again.

And then, almost at the very same instant, he heard that strange sound again.

In the corner of the stall laying on her side was his nanny goat, Marshmallow.

Ed bent down to get a closer look, but his flashlight went out yet again.

As the lightning flashed again, the dark, musty barn was bathed for a few seconds in light.

The light didn't last very long, but it was enough.

For in those brief instances, as the rain kept pounding on the tin barn roof, thunder crackled and the torrential wind threatened to blow the barn down, Ed thought he saw yet another kid cuddled up against Marshmallow.

"Whoa!" he yelled. "What in God's name do we have here?"

CHAPTER 3

A Call To The Doctor

Ed stroked his dog's head as he tried to calm himself next to this unusual (to say the least) newborn baby. Ed lay down on the hay and listened to the roar of the thunder. The strong wind that kept banging against the latched barn doors continued all night.

But the pink and wrinkled baby boy, his eyes shut, and his tiny fists clenched, didn't stir. Ed had removed his coat and gently wrapped the little one in it to guard against the chill. And all night, his faithful dog Denny stayed close to the infant, as if standing guard.

"What the devil are we gonna do with this child, Denny?" Ed asked.

"Why, I'm just barely able to take care of you and myself, let alone a newborn. And what will people think when they see him? Lord God, give me a sign. Tell me what do."

By 5 in the morning, the storm had subsided, and 90 minutes later, the mountain residents of East Tennessee were treated to a spectacular sunrise. Ed took that as a sign that not all was lost.

So, he carried the wrapped-up sleeping little one to the house and laid him ever so carefully into an old wooden crib that Daisy's grandmother had given them as a wedding present. He swaddled the baby in a blanket. When he did that, the baby awakened and began crying loudly.

Ed noticed that he had beautiful brown eyes and just a hint of dark hair on his otherwise smooth, perfectly shaped head.

And the little boy's body—his mouth, nose, hands, fingers, and legs—were what you would expect. All the parts seemed to be there and in good order.

But not so when you got to the infant's feet.

For instead of having ankles and feet, the kicking, now-screaming baby boy had the hooves of a goat.

Ed had seen these unbelievable features last night in the dimly lit barn, but now, in the house light, they were even more pronounced.

"So, my eyes didn't play any tricks on me," he said. "You are a human baby but you're unlike any baby anyone's ever seen."

The startled man walked to the stove and stuck his pinky into a small pan holding water and a baby bottle with milk. Then he turned off the gas burner and touched his arm with the bottle's nipple.

"That oughta be about right, don't ya' think," he said to his dog, lying next to the crib.

When the baby whimpered, demanding to be fed, Ed put the nipple in the hungry one's mouth and the crying stopped as the baby suckled.

"I'll be danged if you weren't starved," Ed proclaimed. He smiled and his dog, now up on four feet, barked loudly.

"Okay, okay. I haven't forgotten about you. Here's your breakfast," Ed said. He filled a pan with dog food near the back door—Denny's favorite place to eat.

After he'd taken care of Denny, Ed dialed seven numbers for Dr. Charles Benson. He knew it was Saturday morning and "Doc," as everyone called him, didn't keep office hours on the weekend.

But if this wasn't a bonafide emergency, then what was?

"This better be good, Ed," said Doc, sounding exasperated. "I'll be right over there but you're making me late for my tee time."

"I'll make it up to you some way," Ed apologized.

*****

Within 30 minutes, the respected physician, one of the few who still made house calls in that part of the state, rapped on Ed's door.

And as he did that, the baby cried harshly.

"Shoosh, Doc. You woke him up," Ed implored as he ushered Doc in.

"Woke who up, Ed? Last I heard, it was just you and your dog living here."

"You won't believe it until you see it for yourself," said Ed, pointing Doc to the crib.

Doc, a squat muscular man with thick eyebrows, prominent sideburns, a reddish nose, and a sharp, pointed chin, sat his medical bag down on the floor and sighed deeply.

"Now I seriously doubt that Ed. There just ain't much in these mountains that I haven't run across."

And that was the truth. Although preferring to keep a low profile, Doc was a major force in the area medical community. Now in his third decade of practicing medicine, he had delivered more babies and treated more illnesses than 99 percent of his peers.

In short, when it came to afflictions, anomalies, or sickness, Doc—who had thinning gray hair and combed the few strands that he had from his left ear to his right one—had just about seen it all.

“Before you take another step toward that crib, I gotta tell you something, Doc. First, you know you’re my best friend and the only person I can trust with what you’re about to see. But you must promise me that this goes to the grave with you. Do we agree on that?”

“Please don’t show me your no-good brother’s body, Ed,” Doc responded, with a hint of a smile.

“It’s nothing like that, Doc. It’s nothing I did.”

“Then let’s just have a quick look see,” said Doc.

“Doc! Say it.”

“Okay, okay. What I am about to see goes to the grave with me.”

“Now what exactly do we have here?” said Doc as he uncovered the baby down to his feet. “Seems to be a perfectly normal little newborn, Ed.” The doctor patted the baby on the back to make him burp, and as he did, the newborn kicked his cover off.

"Why, I've delivered thousands just like him…" but before Doc finished his sentence, he suddenly went dead silent. His jaw dropped and his eyes widened as he stared at the baby's hooves. Doc backed up and sat down in a rocking chair near the crib.

Then he got back up and studied the little one again—this time touching the two-pronged hooves in disbelief.

"Who's the father of this baby…I mean, creature, Ed? And where's its mother?"

"She's in the barn, Doc."

"You're not making any sense, Ed."

CHAPTER 4

Unraveling The Mystery

Ed and Doc Benson sat at Ed's dining room table sipping on coffee as the big yellow lab snoozed at their feet and the baby remained quiet.

"Sorry about your tee time, Doc."

"Guess it just wasn't meant to be, Ed. It's an imperfect world to say the least.

"Now, start at the beginning and tell me where the dickens you think this creature, uh I mean, baby, came from."

Ed took a gulp of his coffee and swallowed hard.

"Remember that goat you brought me a few months ago, Doc, because its owner had passed? The goat was named Marshmallow?

"Well, it turns out Marshmallow was pregnant."

"Good Lord," Doc said. "I should have figured that out. He must have been experimenting on Marshmallow.

"So exactly who was this guy, Doc?"

"Richard—well, folks in these parts knew him as Doctor Richard Jamison—a well respected geneticist who helped a lot of women give birth to a healthy baby. He worked in the New Life Laboratory in Johnson City. But now that I recall, he once said he had a small lab in his garage, and in his spare time, he was trying to clone a goat. Truth be known, he must have been doing a lot more than that. He was evidently doing some kind of in-vitro fertilization with human DNA involved, using the goat as a host.

Doc, shaking his head in disgust, said, "There must have been a side to Richard that I wasn't aware of. I am not sure what he was trying to accomplish, Ed, but it was wrong. It defied the laws of God and nature. However, as wrong as it was, what we have here in William is a true medical miracle, because all the experts have said for years that human DNA and animal DNA are incompatible. And that even if you inserted human sperm into a goat, or into any other animal, yes, it might lead to fertilization, but the cells would never live."

"So, Doc, how did you know this man?"

Doc Benson explained that the two of them had been in med school together, and that Jamison had stayed in school for specialist training for several additional years.

"He went on to be a geneticist, a high paying job."

"How did Dr. Jamison die, Doc?"

"They found him unconscious in his research lab. He'd suffered a massive heart attack. The poor fellow wasn't that old, Ed. To me, he seemed like a nice guy. Brilliant, too. I played golf with him every two weeks."

"Sorry about your friend, Doc."

Meanwhile the baby began whimpering. Ed, expecting as much, fetched another warm bottle of milk from the stove and gently placed the nipple in the baby's mouth.

The doctor stroked his thick mustache and rubbed his eyes.

"This whole thing is just downright incredible and, like you said, if I hadn't seen it with my own eyes, I woulda never believed it. Did you know, my good friend, that a birth like this has only been a myth? Why, this will turn the laws of genetic science on their end. What I'm trying to say, Ed, is that this birth is HISTORIC, and once the news gets out…"

"Stop right there, Doc! That's not going to happen. Remember your sacred promise to take this with you to the grave? Because what kind of life could this little boy have?"

"I don't know, Ed, but what kind of life will he have anyway? Think about it. Some folks'll want to put him in the circus. He could end up in a freak show or worse."

"That's never going to happen, Doc, because what you've seen here stays here—just between us. And William won't be poked and prodded like some kind of animal. I'll raise him like the boy he is."

"So, you've named him William already?"

"That's right. William Edward Anderson, to be exact. Now I'm going to need your help. Are you with me or not?"

"I reckon I gave you my solemn promise, so yes, I'll help you, Ed. Bring him to the clinic tomorrow morning. It's Sunday and no one will be there. I'll do a complete work up on him. Blood, urine, skin, saliva, the whole nine yards. It'll take a few days to get the full results, but we'll soon know a lot more about him."

*****

The next morning, Ed and Doc were inside the Laketon Clinic. It was a small white building. A sign near the front entrance announced the clinic's hours: MON.-FRI. 9 AM-4:30 PM. CLOSED SAT. & SUN.

The two men stared at x-rays on lighted displays mounted on the wall.

"So, what are we looking at exactly, Doc?"

Doc, pointing to the skull, said, "Everything looks fairly normal here and from his neck and chest to his upper and lower legs. But his skull does look a little thicker right here at his forehead. And of course, his ankles and feet are anything BUT NORMAL."

"What about all those tests you ran?"

"Everything looks perfectly normal so far. But I'll know more when I get the full blood work back from the lab."

"Okay, Doc, now what do we do to keep all this covered up?"

"I began working on that last night, Ed. Remember that fishing trip we took last September? You had a one-night stand with a young woman."

Ed interrupted him: "Whoa! Whoa, Doc! What're you sayin'?"

Doc locked eyes with him: "Are you going to be the father of this child or not, Ed?"

"Go ahead, Doc."

"That same young woman showed up at your place very recently, eight months pregnant. Then she went into labor, and you rushed her to the clinic. People at the golf course, some that know you, heard me say that I'd gotten an urgent call from you to leave. She died giving birth at the clinic."

"So, what became of her body, Doc?"

"I've got that covered. Because, as you know, I'm one of the county coroners. So, I pronounced her dead. I had the funeral home send over a cremation casket. We'll seal it shut so it can't be opened. I've already filled out the forms. She'll be cremated tomorrow. Her name was Gloria Jeanne Tucker, and you're listed as the father of her child.

"Didn't you say you named him William something?"

"William Edward Anderson, Doc. But won't that casket need something in it?"

"You raise livestock, Ed. I'm sure you can come up with something."

CHAPTER 5

A Service For The Ashes

Three days later, Ed received a call from the Rev. Marty Hicks and agreed to let his church hold a memorial service for Gloria Jeanne Tucker.

It was to be a simple but dignified ceremony at 2 p.m. the following Tuesday.

As Ed hung up the phone, he glanced out the window and noticed Doc Benson arriving in his station wagon. The good doctor got out of the car clutching a tin box.

"What's that, Doc?"

"It's your girlfriend's ashes, or at least that's what we're sayin' for the record."

Ed said nothing for a few seconds. Then he spoke.

"I shoulda known. I've been gettin' calls from people all over town, offering their condolences. But none from Madge. I even got one from Reverend Hicks, insisting that I have a memorial service for my girlfriend. So that's going to be at his church next Tuesday."

Madge, 45, was a part time cashier at the Laketon Hardware and Grocery, and over the past several months, she and Ed had gotten close. Cute with average height, a head-turning figure, and shoulder length dark hair, Madge had been pursued by many a man in Laketon.

But for whatever reason, she had remained single, and there was just something about Ed that generated sparks between the two.

Not that their paths crossed that often, but when Ed shopped at the Laketon Hardware and Grocery, you could depend on Madge eying him from the time he came in the door till when he left.

One thing had led to another, and they became a couple—but not the marrying kind. Because Madge rather enjoyed having her own space and income and not being tethered to a husband.

"Been there and done that," she confided to Ed early in their relationship. "And don't ask me any questions. For now, let's just enjoy seeing each other."

And from there, whatever they had together progressed quickly. It had started with having coffee together or watching a movie or just going for a walk.

Till one day when Ed stopped by where Madge worked, she had let him know she didn't like going very long without seeing him.

"Where you been, big fella, and how you been doin'?" she asked.

"I'm good, Madge. You know…just a lot of stuff going on lately at the farm. And you?"

"I'm ok," she said, flashing him a sunny smile. Then as she rang up his bag of dog food, she got more serious.

"Why don't you come over tomorrow night about 6? I'll fix you a pot roast."

"Really?" he said, returning her smile. "Hard to say no to your pot roast."

As Ed said his farewell and began to leave, Madge whispered to him.

"And bring your toothbrush."

*****

"Did you really expect Madge to get in touch with you, Ed?" Doc asked. "I know you're really fond of her but just remember, she's a woman and think of how she must be taking this. Women don't like bein' shocked."

"I really like her, Doc," Ed replied sadly. "But now I guess it's over. She'll probably never speak to me again. Maybe even hates me."

Doc, trying to be sympathetic, said something about there being a lot of fish in the ocean, and added, "There's no turning back, Ed. I got William's final blood work back, and he's a healthy kid. No pun intended."

*****

The following Tuesday afternoon, Ed, Reverend Hicks, and about 20 other people gathered to offer their condolences inside Hicks' little white Baptist church.

In front of the pulpit was a table with an urn and a photo of a woman.

Baby William was in a basket in the first pew. Women huddled around him for a close look. He was in a little sleeper jumpsuit, tied like a sack at the bottom to conceal his hooves.

"Ain't you the cutest little thing," one of the mourners gushed.

"And don't he look just like his daddy," another opined.

The Rev. Hicks called for everyone to be seated.

Doc Benson whispered to Ed, "Why is that picture on the table?"

"Because the preacher said I should at least have a picture of my girlfriend by her ashes."

"So, who is the picture of?" Doc asked.

"I don't know," Ed said. "Just some pretty woman. I got it at Walmart. It was in the frame."

The organ music got softer as the Rev. Hicks began his eulogy. He spoke of Gloria Jeanne Tucker being a child of the Almighty God and one that surely had ascended to Heaven.

"And we know, ladies and gentlemen, as we are here to celebrate her too short life on this earth, that each and every one of us has sinned and fallen short of the glory of God."

"She done fooled around and she's a sinner if ever they was one," a bearded old-timer belted out. He leaned on a cane in the back of the church.

Two other stern-faced mourners jumped up from their seats and quickly ushered the man out of the sanctuary.

The interruption caused the Reverend Hicks to temporarily lose his voice. But then the clergyman, who had seen a lot in his years in the church, regained it and continued with his remarks.

"And not only was she a child of God, she was one of His angels. And we are all here today to make sure she's never forgotten. And as to her close friend, Ed Anderson, he has been blessed with a precious little boy.

"Let us know, Ed, if any of us here can help you."

Nods of agreement from the attendees.

After a few more sentences of high praise for the deceased, the minister concluded his eulogy, and all present sang "How Great Thou Art!"

As the throng, many of them dressed in black, filed quietly out of the church, a middle-aged woman clad in what appeared to be her Sunday best approached Ed.

"Wow! That was your girlfriend?" she asked. "I adored her."

"You did," Ed asked.

"Yeah. I saw her in Smoky and the Bandit. But I thought she had married Burt Reynolds."

Doc overheard that, and, looking at a picture of Sally Field, he glanced around and purposely bumped the table with his hip. That knocked the picture to the floor and broke it. He quickly picked up the pieces, including the photograph, and stuffed them in his coat pocket.

After the woman left, Doc confronted Ed.

"My God, Ed. Don't you know who Sally Field is?"

"I do now. She was my girlfriend."

*****

The next day, Ed stopped at the Laketon Hardware and Grocery to buy flour, sugar, coffee, formula, diapers, and baby food.

Leaving William in a basket on the front seat of the truck with Denny watching over him, Ed entered the store. As Ed approached the register with the items he needed, he came eye to eye with Madge.

"You're not fooling me for a second, Ed Anderson," Madge whispered to him. "You might have all those other folks fooled, but I know that isn't your baby. Because I know you like the back of my hand. But why all the charades?

"It's complicated, Madge. But plea.."

Madge interrupted him: "You don't have to worry. Your secret is safe with me, Ed. Call me if you need help with the baby. I know about babies."

After paying for the items, Ed started for the door.

Ed blew her a kiss and promised he'd be in touch.

"Oops, I forgot something, Madge. Poor Denny is feeling neglected. Where y'all keeping your dog toys these days?"

"We got a new shipment a couple of days ago. Take a look in the far back of the store on the left side of aisle 12."

Ed, nodding, laid his groceries down on the counter and told Madge he'd only be a minute. Once he reached aisle 12, he noticed an attractive woman stocking the shelves. She helped him find the dog toys and then he shook her hand.

"I haven't seen you before, have I," Ed asked.

Ann Smith, 28, with long brown hair, brown eyes and perfect teeth, paused from what she was doing, introduced herself, and told Ed that she had just started working the previous day. She then asked him about his dog and soon learned that the two of them shared a love for canines.

"So, where you from, Ann?" Ed noticed that her casual V-neck tee-shirt revealed a hint of enticing cleavage.

"Atlanta."

Ed, laughing, told her that he had once been lost there and spent two days in Spaghetti Junction. "Then I finally ditched my car and hitch hiked back to Tennessee."

Ann handed him a pack of snacks for his dog Denny and smiled. Then she confessed to not knowing much about Laketon or East Tennessee—having ended up here to care for her ailing 92-year-old great aunt. Ann said she decided to stay after her aunt passed away six months later.

Ed assured her that she had made a good decision in staying. "You'll like it here, Ann. It's slow paced, folks are friendly, and we have the mountains, Watauga Lake—one of the cleanest lakes in America—the Cherokee National Forest, and the A.T."

When Ann asked him what he meant by the 'A.T.,' Ed explained that was shorthand for the Appalachian Trail—one of the best hiking trails in America.

"Runs from Georgia to Maine and it just so happens that we've got a good stretch of it in these mountains in our very own little community. In fact, part of the trail skirts my farm."

As he was about to turn to leave, Ann noticed that he had three boxes of cookies. When she remarked that he must really like cookies, Ed said, "Oh, they're not for me. They're for my kids."

"And so, how many kids do you have?"

"Two," he said. "I had three, but I just sold one yesterday."

Puzzled and raising her eyebrows, she said, "Oh really? So how much does a good kid sell for these days?"

"Well, for the boys, usually forty or fifty dollars," Ed said, "but the girls can fetch as much as one-hundred and fifty."

"Makes sense to me," she replied.

"So very nice meeting you, Ann. I'm in here from time to time. Madge and I are good friends. I'll let her know that you waited on me and gave me excellent service."

Ann thanked him and said she would definitely check out the 'A.T.'

CHAPTER 6

Visit From A Wayward Member Of The Family

The next morning started out as a typical East Tennessee spring day full of sunshine, a mountain breeze, blooming flowers, and chirping birds.

Ed rose early, made himself a steaming hot cup of coffee, changed and fed William, and spent a few minutes stroking his best four-legged friend—Denny.

"Let's you and me get some things accomplished today," he said.

After checking again on William, man and dog made their way to the barn where Ed had a woodworking shop.

On his work bench was a whirligig—a little wooden man with swinging arms and legs that was attached to a mechanism with a wood propeller on the opposite end.

When Ed spun the propeller with his finger, the brightly painted man began dancing.

Ed sat there enjoying his handiwork for a few minutes while Denny, seemingly always up for a nap, lay next to him.

But a horn honking in the driveway aroused the big dog. His ears suddenly in an upward position and the fur on his back standing up, Denny barked loudly.

"What's got you all riled up?" Ed asked.

He peeked through a crack in the barn door and noticed a yellow Cadillac convertible in the driveway next to his house.

"Now who the devil might that be?" Ed, aggravated, wondered aloud. He exited the shop, his protective dog trotting closely behind him.

It was none other than Buzz Dawson, Ed's stepbrother.

Tall and lanky with scraggly black hair, a ruddy complexion, and a tattoo of a skull on his neck, Ed last heard Buzz lived near Panama City, Florida. Ed hardly ever saw him and when he did it was usually bad news.

"I'm surprised to see you, Buzz. What brings to Laketon?"

Hugging him, Buzz flashed a big smile showing his front gold tooth. Then he slapped Ed on his right shoulder and said he had meant to visit more often but life had been hectic.

"I just wanted to see my big brother!"

"Stepbrother, Buzz," Ed corrected him. "Last I heard, you were livin' with a woman and her 5-year-old son. You end up marryin' her?"

"Not hardly! That bitch threw me out years ago. She wanted to wear the pants, and I've been with another woman since then. But damned if she didn't start cheatin' on me! I caught her and guess what? She threw me out, too!"

"So, she kicked you out of her house and now your homeless?" Ed asked. "And how in God's name can you afford that fancy car?"

"That vehicle is a 1955 El Dorado, a classic, and it's another story, but yep, big brother, she threw me outta her house two days ago. Said she'd call the law and tell them I beat her up if I didn't scat right away. Which was a lie."

"So now you come draggin' in here with your tail between your legs wantin' to stay here? Is that about right, Buzz?"

"I just need a place to stay for a few days—till I can figure out my next move. I promise I won't be no bother, big brother."

"And you'll stay away from the bottle. I'm not puttin' up with a drunk, Buzz. The first time you come in smellin' of alcohol and raisin' hell, you're outta here. You understand?"

"I don't do that no more, big brother."

*****

Late one day the following week, Ed had been invited by Madge to have pot roast with her again—and to again bring his toothbrush.

"And bring William and Denny with you," she said. "They won't be any trouble."

Ed had anticipated being invited to Madge's again and he was well aware of how hard it would be to keep her from seeing little William's hooves. And not only Madge, but with anyone, there was always that risk. One slip and William's life would have been changed forever.

So, Ed and Doc came up with a plan. The story would go like this: (Doc sent Ed with William to a podiatrist in Johnson City because little William's feet were not straight. They pointed inward. The podiatrist fitted little high-top corrective baby shoes on William that he would wear 24-7. This would make his feet grow straight and keep him from needing surgery. The only time the shoes were to come off was when he was bathed. Then Ed went shopping and managed to find a pair of little baby shoes that worked just fine).

Madge lived about two miles away in a little house with a picket fence. Giant oak trees framed the driveway and daffodils gave the property more than a splash of brilliant color.

After dinner, Ed and Madge sat in rocking chairs on her front porch with William in his basket beside them. Denny snoozed near the basket. They made small talk, held hands, and then later adjourned to Madge's king size 4-poster bed. They had put William in the extra bedroom.

"I forgot to bring my pajamas. Sorry," Ed said as Madge emerged from the bathroom in a tantalizing pink negligee.

"I like skin and lots of it," she said.

"And I like a woman who knows what she wants."

*****

Later, exhausted from their activity between the sheets, they slept— then awakened in each other's arms.

Madge got up and checked on William and found Denny at the foot of the bed. Then she returned to the bed and cuddled up next to Ed.

"Everything okay?" Ed asked.

"Everything is fine. William is sound asleep and his protecter is on the foot of the bed. But I hate that he has to wear those shoes all the time. Poor little fellow."

Ed said, "I know, but it will keep him from needing surgery later."

"He's such a good baby, Ed. A blessing for you, I'm sure. I'll need to bathe him in the morning. After all, he's already been through three diapers since you got here."

"Not necessary, Madge. Because for one thing, I'll have to be gettin' out of here at first light. And for another, Denny has an appointment at the vet at 9 in the morning. Time for his rabies shot."

"Okay," Madge said, disappointed.

Madge looked at Ed seductively, batting her long eye lashes.

"So did you like my pot roast?"

“Madge, you know I devoured it.”

“And?” she asked him.

“And everything else,” he said

She gave him a disgusted look and he squirmed.

“You’re a typical man. Takin’ everything a woman has to offer and leavin’ the first chance you get.”

“You know I love you, Madge.” He followed up with a long, wet kiss, and the couple fell asleep again.

*****

The next afternoon, Ed stopped at the Laketon Hardware and Grocery, leaving William in a basket on the truck seat with Denny beside him.

“Mornin’, Ann,” he said, as he entered the store.

“Needin’ some more cookies?”

“No, not this trip. But I do need a box of finishing nails.”

Ann pointed him toward the hardware side of the store, and within a few minutes, Ed came back with a box of nails and a small can of red paint.

“I met your brother yesterday,” she said. “He can be quite charming.”

“Yes, he can be.”

Give him a chance and he’ll charm you right out of your pants, Ed thought.

“Actually, he’s my stepbrother, Ann.”

“Guess what? He’s going to take me out to dinner.”

“He can be nice when he wants to, Ann. Hope y’all have a good time.”

But as Ed drove away in his truck, he had his doubts. Because, for whatever reason, some women were attracted to Buzz, and he always did them wrong.

When he got home, he found Buzz lazing in the porch swing.

“Hey, Buzz. That new gal at the grocery store told me you’re taking her out to dinner.”

“Ann? Yep. She’s a fox, ain’t she?”

“She’s a lady, too, Buzz, and don’t you forget that. I want you to treat her like one. You have enough money to take her someplace nice?”

When his stepbrother didn't respond right away, Ed could tell he'd hit a nerve.

"Well, of course I do. You think I'd ask her out if I didn't?"

"I just don't want her to get hurt or be embarrassed, Buzz. And you don't have the best track record with women. By the way, you might want to wear a turtleneck shirt to cover up that tattoo. That skull is not the most flattering thing."

Buzz, staring at the ground, stayed silent for a few seconds and gripped his elbows.

"You know, now that you mention it, I could use a few more dollars. That is, if you could see fit to help me out. I promise I'll pay you back when I get more settled."

Like he'll really keep that promise. I won't be holding my breath, Ed thought.

When Ed agreed to his request, instead of thanking him, Buzz became more emboldened. And, as if to flaunt his nastiness, he showed both his fists—each knuckle with a letter spelled out LOVE on his left hand and HATE on his right.

"Lovely," said Ed sarcastically.

"You know, big brother, I feel like I have an interest in this farm. After all, I was a son."

"A stepson," Ed said. "You came here when your mom married Dad. You were 15, and before your mom passed—bless her heart—we promised her we'd make you a part of this family. And we tried.

"But what did you do? You dropped out of school and started carousin' and drinkin' and kept getting arrested and thrown in jail."

"I wasn't good at taking that medicine the doctor gave me, Ed. I couldn't help it. I couldn't stand the taste of it."

Ed had heard that same excuse countless times.

"Then what did you do? You just up and left and we gave up trying to find you."

"Well, I did send y'all a post card," Buzz said meekly. "It wasn't like I flew the coop and kept y'all in the dark."

"You wrote to us saying you were living in Florida. How you got down there or who took you I guess we'll never know, but I do know this. You'd have been in Dad's will if you had stayed here on the farm and done your part."

"And what in tarnation did you do, big brother, that you're so high and mighty today?"

Ed tightened his jaws and grimaced, "I'll tell you what I did. I worked this farm—till I was bone tired every night—with Dad for 15 years. And if you remember, when he died, I offered to give you an interest in the property if you'd come back and help me. But no, you never returned, and you didn't even come and pay your respects at Dad's funeral."

Buzz didn't flinch this time as he looked Ed in the eye and said, "It was that damned medicine. I couldn't stand the taste of it. Plus, I had a lot of things going on, Ed, and I just couldn't get up and leave. But the bottom line is, I still think I deserve something. I'm broke. Dead broke. And big brother, the bitch I was livin' with took all the money out of our bank account and made me homeless. I had to sell stuff just to pay for the gas to get me here."

"So, you thought you'd come crawlin' back here and live off me for a while? That about, right?"

This time, Buzz screamed his words.

"For God's sake, Ed, I'm your brother! We grew up together. Slept in the same room. Ate the same food. Did the same chores. Is a little help from your brother asking too much?!"

“Stepbrother, Buzz. And you had your chance and didn’t take it. But I’ll tell you what. You can stay here a month. Then you’re on your own.

“Now here’s a little cash to take Ann out.” Ed opened his wallet and pulled out sixty dollars. “If you want more, you’ll have to earn it.”

Without saying thanks, Buzz eagerly clutched the money and stuffed it into his billfold.

“So, where you planning to take her, if I may ask?”

“Well, now, that ain’t none of your business! Seems ta’ me you got enough on your plate with a new bastard baby, all the work on this farm, and that sexy woman at the store you shack up with every now and then.”

“Watch your mouth!” Ed said sternly. “Or you’ll find yourself sleepin’ in that Cadillac!”

*****

In the following weeks, Ed worked Buzz hard. Ed had him up at 5 a.m., fed, and working by 6. Buzz mowed and bailed hay and hauled and muscled it into the barn. And when he wasn’t doing that, he was mending fences.

Always one who despised getting out of bed so early, Buzz nevertheless stayed the course. Because he knew if he didn't, he'd be kicked out.

And he kept reminding himself that he had no other place to live.

So, he worked for Ed from 6 a.m. to 5 p.m. five days a week with Saturday and Sunday off. And when he was off, he spent most of his time with Ann.

It was as if, early in their relationship, he couldn't get enough of her.

He started showing up at Laketon Grocery and Hardware 30 minutes before she got off work at 6 p.m. to drive her home, which was only a short walk.

Buzz treated her well, often bringing her flowers and writing sweet notes he had copied from women's magazines.

Then he got extremely possessive, telling her, after a few weeks he didn't want her having anything to do with anyone else.

"All we need is each other," Buzz said (again stealing a line from a magazine). "We're soulmates; I knew it the day I met you. So, what I want you to promise me is you won't be so nice to men customers because they'll think you're flirting with them and take advantage of you."

Ann, not used to being so controlled by another person, was uncomfortable with Buzz's command. But she agreed to it, reminding herself that for all his faults, this strange, and in some ways wild man—who had seemingly appeared from nowhere—was good to her.

*****

A couple of weeks later, Ed was on his way back from Johnson City with a part for his hay bailer. William was in his basket on the seat of his truck and Denny sat by the door.

Ed stopped at Laketon Hardware and Grocery to pick up a few things.

"Stay, Denny," Ed told his obedient dog as he left the vehicle and went inside.

Pete, the store owner, a tall thin man with thin gray hair and a mustache, was standing near the door as Ed entered.

"Hi, Pete. How you doin'?"

"I've had better days, Ed."

Got to remember to ask him what's up with him on my way out, Ed thought.

He picked up a box of cookies and a quart of milk and walked to the register where Ann was standing with her head turned to the side.

"Hi, Ann. How are you?"

Ann answered, "Fine" without looking at him and began ringing him up.

Ed touched her chin and turned her face to where he could see it.

She had a bulging black eye and an ugly purple bruise on her cheek.

She turned so as to hide her wounds and started to cry.

"That'll be four dollars and twenty-five cents, Ed."

"My God, Ann! Did Buzz do that to you?"

No response.

"Ann! Did Buzz do that to you?"

Ann said (sobbing), "I was just trying to be nice to a young man. He said I was flirting."

Ed laid down a 5-dollar bill and stormed out the door. He got in his truck and spun the tires pulling onto the highway. Then he looked down at William and slowed down.

Pete watched Ed pull away. *I sure wouldn't want to be Buzz right now,* he thought.

Minutes later, Ed pulled in his driveway and slid to a stop, holding the basket with William.

Not seeing Buzz's car, he slammed his fist on the dashboard scaring William, which made him feel terrible.

Inside the house, he gently set the basket with William on the kitchen table. Then, still trying to control his anger, he turned his attention to Buzz's room. Drawers were open and empty, as was the closet.

Ed returned to the kitchen as the phone mounted on the wall started ringing.

"Hello. Tell her I'm fine, Pete, and she doesn't have to worry anymore. Buzz flew the coop."

When Pete mentioned that Buzz recently paid for some merchandise with a check, Ed assured him that he (Ed) would cover it.

Pete said that wouldn't be necessary, adding that he would gladly accept the lost funds if only Buzz would leave his employee alone.

"No, I want to, Pete. I'll stop by tomorrow."

Ed hung up and plopped down in a kitchen chair.

Denny, sensing his master was troubled, laid his head in Ed's lap and licked his right hand.

"Never again, Denny. Never again," he said as he stroked the dog's head.

*****

Gradually, life became a little more normal in the following weeks. With so much work always to be done on the farm, there wasn't much time to fret over Buzz, where he might be, or what he might be up to.

Tasks, whether they involved livestock, hay, fences, or any of the other many things that awaited attention, demanded Ed's full energy and concentration. And if they didn't get done one day, he woke up to them the next.

On a cool summer evening, after feeding and bathing William, Ed carried his little son in his basket to the front porch. He sat down in his favorite rocker and sat William beside him on the floor. Then he lit his pipe that he smoked occasionally.

Ed wondered how he would navigate his and William's life in the coming months and years. He knew it wouldn't be easy.

On nice days when Ed worked the farm, he would take William with him. If it was raining or too cool, Ed left him in the house and made trips back every few hours. When Ed went to town—whether it was to a store, post office, gas station, friend's house or wherever—William went.

The two were practically one.

Ed finally got some help when he later found a woman who had a daycare in Laketon. Mrs. Mooney had strict instructions to never remove William's corrective shoes because he had a medical problem.

That is what Ed told her and Mrs. Mooney never questioned it.

As Ed started nodding off and almost dropped his pipe, he was startled wide awake. A baby blue VW Beetle had pulled to a stop in the driveway near the porch. Ann exited the car and walked toward the porch. Danny ran to greet her.

"Ann, how nice. How'd you find me?"

"Pete told me where you lived, Ed. It's beautiful here."

"Me and William like it. Come and sit on the porch, Ann."

That's when she noticed William.

"Oh! There's that handsome boy."

Ann sat down on the porch swing.

"He's asleep, Ed. Let's not wake him."

Then she turned serious.

"Can we talk a few minutes, Ed?"

"Of course, Ann. What's the problem?"

"I need to get in touch with Buzz. I'm pregnant and Buzz is the father. I'm going to live with my mother so she can help me. But she doesn't have any money. Buzz needs to help."

"Buzz would never give you a cent, Ann. All he'd do is make your life a living hell."

"But I—"

Ed interrupted her.

"I will help you, Ann."

"That's not your responsibility, Ed. Why would you do that?"

She cried as Ed hugged her and said he'd be right back with something for her. As he went inside, Denny nuzzled his head in Ann's lap, and she petted him. Ed came back a few minutes later and handed Ann a check.

"This is too much, Ed. I can't accept this."

He hugged her again and told her it was for her and her baby to be. And then he made her promise him that she would stay away from Buzz for the rest of her life.

"How can I ever repay you?" asked a teary-eyed Ann.

"By living a good life and staying in touch, Ann. Send me a picture every now and then and let me know how you're doin'."

"God bless you, Ed."

CHAPTER 7

An Act Of Kindness

Five years later, Ed took a ride in his pickup truck to the back end of his property—which was between Pond Mountain and Watauga Lake—with its 104 miles of cliff-lined shoreline and quiet coves.

It was a wooded area that he rarely visited, but occasionally he'd go there with Denny and William to meditate and take in the wonders of nature.

While he already had a few cows, he dreamed one day of having a larger herd grazing on the spacious grassy pastures. It would be the perfect place for cattle or even goats, he figured, because that part of his farm had two spring-fed ponds that never went dry.

He made his way through the tall, lush grass to an overgrown with weeds and trees primitive log house that his grandfather had built. He pushed the creaking door open and noticed a big black snake coiled up and blocking the entrance to the decrepit structure's only bedroom. Ed hissed at the snake, but it refused to move. So, he picked up a tree limb and nudged the reptile little by little till it was outside.

Back inside, Ed surveyed the house and noticed it was full of cobwebs, rat feces, and cockroaches. But the floor and walls were in fairly good shape, considering they were likely more than a century old and no one had lived here for so long.

He thought it was a shame that the place—the starter home for Ed's dad's parents—was in such shambles, but he didn't have the time or energy to improve it.

As fate would have it, later that same day, he happened upon a big, strapping muscular Black man who was repairing a wire fence which separated Ed's farm from a neighbor's land. The man, who appeared to be about 50 years old, had a prosthetic left leg from the knee down and was shirtless with camouflage cargo-style pants. A young, wide-eyed boy sat on a stump a few feet away.

"How ya doing and what's your name, big fella," Ed yelled from the rolled down window of his pickup truck.

"John Washington," the man with ivory white teeth and a beautiful smile yelled back. "I be doin' some fence work for Mister and Mizzus Robinson.

"Well, glad to meet you, John. My name's Ed Anderson. Who's that fine looking young lad that's with you?"

John smiled broadly and said that was his 5-year-old son Raymond.

"That right, John? Just so happens my son William is the same age. He's back at my house right now but maybe he and Raymond could be friends."

"That'd be good, Mister Ed."

Weeks went by and Ed continued to bump into John and his son. The two men always took time to exchange pleasantries and trade stories about their sons. Ed learned that John had stepped on a booby trap while in combat in the Vietnam War in the late 1960s.

One late afternoon, John was riding along a back road from his farm into Laketon. He spotted John and his boy walking in the woods next to the road. The big Black man had what appeared to be a bedroll on his back. His son toted a small bag stuffed with clothes.

"Hey there, John! Where y'all going?"

"We be on our way tryin' to find some place to camp, Mister Ed. Mister and Missuz Robinson ain't got no more work for us and so we cain't stay in their barn no more."

"So you tellin' me you and your son don't have a home, John?"

"We did have till my wife done kicked us out. Found herself another man and said she wasn't takin' care of no youngun' no more. And let me know she didn't want half a man for a husband no more."

"I see. You and Raymond throw your things in the back of my truck and come take a ride with me," Ed said.

"Where we goin', Mr. Ed?" said the surprised big man, his little son in tow.

Within a few minutes they were on the back side of Ed's farm.

"This was my grandparents' old homeplace. My grandfather built it," Ed explained as they all got out of the pickup truck and walked toward the still standing unkempt old structure shaded by towering tulip poplar trees.

"Nobody's lived here for years, except for a long time ago a young couple talked me into renting it to them. They trashed it, so I ran them off and it's been empty ever since.

"How would you and Raymond like to live here, John?"

"How much would the rent be, Mr. Ed?"

"Tell you what, John. You pay for the electric and do some paintin' and fixin' up in your spare time and help me around the farm every now and then. That'll be your rent. It has a good well and a good cast iron stove for heat. Deal?"

John extended his hand, and the two shook on it.

"Deal, Raymond," Ed said.

The little kid giggled with delight.

"Let me show you inside, John, before it gets too dark."

CHAPTER 8

Spilling The Beans

Four months later, Ed had an appointment with Dr. Randolph Mills, an optometrist in Elizabethton, just a few miles down the road from Laketon.

He had been in the waiting room for almost an hour when he rose and asked the receptionist if he could use the office telephone.

When she said yes, he dialed Madge's home number.

"Hi, Madge. It's me. Sorry to bother you."

"It's no trouble, Ed. I took the day off from work today so I could clean my house."

Ed told her where he was—in Elizabethton getting new eyeglasses—and said he would be running a bit late in getting back home.

"I won't be back when the school bus brings the kids home. They can entertain themselves, Madge, but I need somebody there. John is working on the back side of the farm, and I can't reach him or else he could be there with them, so I was wondering…"

"Just stop right there, Ed. You know you don't even have to ask me. I love those two kids."

Ed breathed a sigh of relief as the receptionist gave him a look that he shouldn't tie up the phone line much longer.

"Thanks a bunch, Madge," he said enthusiastically. "And Madge, have dinner with us. And bring your toothbrush."

Realizing the receptionist had overheard him as he handed the phone back to her, Ed thanked the officious woman and gave her a half smile.

*****

Later that same afternoon, William and Raymond were climbing on the John Deere tractor parked under an overhang on the side of the barn. Denny, who never strayed far from William, barked when the two rambunctious boys made motor noises and pretended to drive.

Suddenly, William saw a small bunny scamper under the tractor, and he jumped down, trying to catch it.

At that same time, Raymond pretended to steer. He pulled the gear shift lever—which popped the tractor out of gear.

As a result, the tractor rolled forward a couple of feet and pinned one of William's feet under the back wheel.

Only the top of his boot was visible.

"Help me, Raymond! I can't pull my foot out!"

Raymond climbed down from the tractor and pulled on William's leg.

"It won't come out, William. Doesn't it hurt?"

"No. Go get Miss Madge, Raymond. She can help me."

Madge had just finished making peanut butter sandwiches in the kitchen for the kids' lunch. She stepped to the back door and hollered for them.

"William, Raymond! Come and get your lunch!"

Raymond ran in, sat down at the kitchen table, and took a big bite of his sandwich.

"I love peanut butter, Miss Madge."

"Raymond, where is William? Wasn't he with you?"

"Oh yea. William wants you to help him, Miss Madge. That tractor ran over his foot, and he can't get it out."

"Oh my God!" Madge screamed.

Thinking William had probably been severely injured, she gasped, dropped what she was doing, and rushed outside toward the tractor.

When she got there, she saw William's foot, turned backwards and apparently smashed under the tractor's back wheel, which terrified her.

"Hang on, William! I'll help you!"

"It's okay, Miss Madge. It don't hurt. Dad can fix it."

With that, Madge leaned hard with her back against the rear tractor wheel and nudged the tractor just enough that William could pull free.

Then, fighting tears, she scooped William up and ran back toward the house.

"It'll be okay. You're going to be all right," she told William repeatedly and nervously as Denny barked alongside her.

"I know, Miss Madge. Dad can fix it."

She sat William down in a chair in the living room and instructed Raymond to stay with him as she called Ed.

But the call wasn't necessary because Ed himself walked in the door.

"Thank God you're home and just in the nick of time," said Madge, panic in her voice. "We need to get William to the hospital. His foot was crushed under the tractor."

"It's okay, Miss Madge. Dad can fix it," William said again.

Meanwhile, Raymond kept taking bites out of his peanut butter sandwich.

"He be okay, Miss Madge," said Raymond, his mouth stuffed full of food.

"Now you listen to me, Raymond," Madge snapped. "You boys didn't have any business playin' on that tractor anyway. IT IS NOT A TOY!"

Ed, taking it all in, said, "Calm down, Madge, and sit down. And you, William, stay right where you are for now."

William stuck the leg straight out and the toe of his boot dropped, pointing to the floor.

"Yep, Dad. I think I broke my foot."

Madge gasped again. "My God, Ed! His foot was turned backwards. We have to take him to the hospital right now!"

But Ed tried to persuade her that William didn't need medical treatment.

"He's not hurt that bad, Madge. Because he doesn't seem to be in pain. Just calm down. You stay with Raymond. I'll take care of William."

William looked at the eccentric Madge and assured her his dad would take good care of him.

"I don't need to go to the hospital, Miss Madge, because I have special feet. Dad can fix my broken one."

Madge, looking confused, eyeballed Ed and demanded that he tell her what was going on with his son.

"What does William mean when he says Dad can fix it and that he has special feet?"

Exasperated and with his son in his arms, Ed said, "We'll talk about it when we get back. But I need to take William with me to the barn."

That didn't sit well with Madge, who said sternly, "Ed Anderson, if you go out that door, I'm going out this one and don't expect me to ever come back. I'M TIRED OF ALL THIS SECRECY ABOUT WILLIAM'S SPECIAL FEET! Now you be straight with me and tell me what's going on. Because I love that boy like he's my own."

When Ed didn't respond, Madge insisted that he come clean.

"Do you really think that if he has some kind of deformity, I'll love him any less?"

"Wait, Miss Madge," William pleaded. "Dad, don't let her go. Please!"

Ed looked forlornly at Madge gathering up her things and headed toward the front door. Then he turned around and saw Raymond, holding his peanut butter sandwich, standing in the doorway.

"Raymond, go outside, son, until we call you back in."

After Raymond had left, Ed put William back down in a chair and bent down and began unlacing his boots.

"William, look at me son. We're going to let Miss Madge see your special feet. But nobody else. Understand?"

"Yes sir, because I love Miss Madge. And nobody'll know except for you, me, Doc, and Miss Madge. Right, Dad?"

"That's right, son. Now take your boots off."

The little boy did as he was asked, removing the boot from his completely turned around, broken wooden foot. And there, revealed for everyone to see, was his two-pronged hoof.

"That's what I thought, Dad. My foot broke off."

Madge, shocked, said nothing and at first covered her eyes.

But after several seconds, she got up from her chair and walked over and touched William's hoof.

"I know now why you call them special feet, William. Because they are indeed very special," she said tearfully.

Then, turning to Ed, she told him she had a few questions.

"We can talk about that tonight," he said. "It's a long story. Now please put your overnight bag back down. We don't want you to leave."

With that, he slipped William's hoof back into the boot and laced it tightly so it would stay straight.

"Go sit out back with Raymond, son. And just sit. Don't play, okay? I want to talk with Miss Madge for a few minutes. Then we'll go to the shop and work on your foot."

William hugged Madge and his dad and left the house.

"So, you've been keeping this a deep dark secret from me for how long," she asked.

"I felt I had to—to protect William," he said.

"And so, you and Doc Benson promised not to tell anyone else?"

Ed said: "It was all so that William could have as normal a life as possible. We did what we thought was right."

"And who is the father, Ed?"

"I have no idea, Madge. But again, it's a long story. Let's start at the beginning."

CHAPTER 9

The Snake Preacher

The best thing that could have happened to William as he got older was to have a good friend like Raymond. The two boys were inseparable—going to school together, playing with the baby goats together on the farm, doing their chores like gathering eggs, shoulder to shoulder.

"Why you so white," Raymond asked him one day. He was light-skinned, like his dad, had a pug nose, and reddish black hair.

"I don't rightly know. But why're you so black," the blond-haired William shot back.

The two boys rolled their eyes, laughed, and began kicking a soccer ball—their favorite past time when they weren't eating, doing homework, or helping their dads.

Minutes earlier in the house, William, with the help of his father, had slipped on his new high-top boots. They covered his hooves nicely and Ed had laced them tight—the better to mask the tapping sound made by the hooves when William walked across a hardwood floor.

"Do you remember what I told you about your special feet, Son?" (Ed had been reminding his son of this for the past two years).

"Yes sir. Nobody can ever see them but you and Doctor Benson—and now Miss Madge. And I can never go outside without my boots on."

"Smart boy, Son."

Later, as William and Raymond kicked the soccer ball, Ed took it all in, relaxing in his rocking chair on the front porch. From there, he had a grand view of Watauga Lake—which on this Saturday was teeming with sailboats, houseboats, and just people out to have a good time on one of Tennessee's most gorgeous TVA lakes.

As the boys played, a car pulled up in the driveway and a short balding man with a substantial pot belly got out and walked toward the porch.

"Good evening, Sir. I am Milford Smith, the new pastor at New Life Baptist Church.

Ed had heard talk around town that Pastor Smith had once been a Pentecostal, rattlesnake-handling preacher in the mountains of Kentucky. Rumor had it that when a member of Smith's congregation picked up a deadly, angry serpent during a church service, it had sunk its venomous fangs into the man's neck. The result was an almost instant, painful death—creating turmoil in that Southern Appalachian community and resulting in Smith's resignation.

But Ed didn't bring up any of this during the pastor's unexpected visit—choosing instead to remain polite and cordial.

"Good evening, Pastor Smith. Come on up on the porch. Have a seat and take a load off," Ed beckoned him. "I'm Ed Anderson and that's my son William and his friend Raymond."

"They look like fine young men," said the pastor, extending his hand to Ed.

"I agree. William's the love of my life, and Raymond is right up there, too. Now what brings you to our farm, Pastor?"

"I just wanted to invite you to our church, Ed. And we have a Sunday School for little ones like William and Raymond.

"Actually, we've been going to the Freewill Baptist church where Reverend Marty Hicks preaches, and we also have a Sunday school for little ones. But thank you for the invite, Pastor Smith."

As the two men chatted, William kicked his soccer ball around the yard while Denny pursued it.

The pastor glanced every now and then at William and noticed that on one occasion when he kicked the ball, his foot turned to its side. And to the pastor's surprise, he witnessed the boy reaching down and turning it back straight. Then, when William kicked the ball again, his foot turned the other way, and William straightened it. He kicked the ball yet again and his foot turned facing backwards.

As William sat down in the grass to work on his foot, the pastor thought he might have been hallucinating. *I didn't really see that boy turn his foot completely around, did I?*

"Man, little kids are really limber, aren't they?" the pastor said.

Ed nodded his agreement.

The pastor replied: "Well, I reckon I best be gettin' along. Tell Reverend Hicks I said hi. I met him. He's a good man."

As the pastor pulled out of the driveway, Ed thought, *I need to do some serious work on that boy's feet.*

*****

In the barn, while William sat on a stool, Ed held one of this son's hooves on a belt sander. Within a few minutes, he slipped William's hoof inside the hollowed out, wooden foot he had crafted. Then he did something he had not done in the past. He inserted screws on three sides—careful not to let the screws go too deep. Ed assumed this would hold William's feet straight.

"We're almost finished, William. You've been very patient with me."

"Yeah, I know, Dad. Do other kids have special feet like mine?"

"I don't think so, son. There now. Let's slip your boots on."

"Dad, why did God want me to have special feet anyway?"

"I'm not sure, William. But I'm certain he had a good reason. How do your feet feel now?"

William said his feet were good and asked to go back outside and play with Raymond.

*****

A few days later, as the sun was within an hour of dipping below the mountain top that cast a shadow on a good portion of Ed's property, Ed pulled up in a field near the house. He was on a Ford tractor pulling a wagon stacked with square bales of hay. Numerous other bales of hay were on the ground in rows.

With the wagon loaded with two layers of bales, Ed struggled to pile them any higher. And seeing several failed attempts, Ed hollered loudly for John to come out of the barn and help him.

The strapping muscular John heaved the heavy bales up as Ed stacked them.

Eventually, thanks to the efforts of John, the wagon was stacked with six layers of hay.

"Wagon's full, Mr. Ed," John hollered.

"Okay, John. I'm heading to the barn."

*****

The following day, Ed and John arrived in his pickup truck in a grassy pasture with about 30 black angus cattle. The curious animals watched them closely as they got out of the vehicle, climbed on the tailgate, and began unraveling baling twine from the hay. Then the two men heaved bales of hay down to the ground.

It was hard, demanding, sweaty, back-breaking work but the men continued with their heaving till all the hay was off the truck.

"Here you go, John," Ed said, handing his friend two twenty-dollar bills. "Good job. Now go wash up and I'll fix us something to eat."

"No, Mr. Ed. I work fo' my rent. You not supposed to pay me."

"You have worked really hard the last couple of days, John, and so I intend to pay you when you do that."

"But Mr. E—"

"End of discussion, John. I'm the boss."

"Yes Sir," said John with a smile.

CHAPTER 10

Sneaking A Peek

The following day was a Saturday, so Ed slept a little later as did William. Ed sat in the kitchen and read the local newspaper Denny had brought him from the front yard, while enjoying a hot cup of coffee. At about 8, he went in and shook William.

"Get up, Son, put on your clothes and boots and come in the kitchen. How about some pancakes and sausage for breakfast?"

"Yeah. That's what I want, Dad. I love pancakes and sausage."

"Okay, hurry up. Raymond will probably be coming over soon."

A short time later Ed had the sausage made and the pancakes on the griddle, and William was still in his bedroom.

"Where are you, William?"

Ed heard the clack, clack, clack, as William entered the kitchen holding his boots.

"I can't get my boots on, Dad. They're too tight."

“Okay. Sit in the chair, son, and I’ll help you.”

Ed managed to get William’s boots on, but he understood why it would be a struggle for the little fellow. He realized he needed to shave a little wood off the wooden feet to make it easier for William.

“Eat your breakfast, son. Then you can go to the shop and I can fix ’em for you.”

“Oh no. Not again,” William said, putting his hands on top of his head.

“It won’t take that long, son. I promise.”

“What if Raymond comes?”

“Then he can just wait,” Ed said.

And indeed, that’s what happened.

Raymond sat in a swing that hung in a tree near the back of the house while Ed and William were in the barn shop.

But before Ed started working, he thought it would be a good idea to take one last glance out the barn window and check on Raymond—just to make sure he was still in the swing. So, he stepped up on a foot stool and looked outside. Raymond was swinging away. So Ed stepped back down and started sanding on one of the wooden feet with a small hand sander, while William sat in a chair, his hoofs sticking straight out.

Then, as luck would have it, out of the past came Ed's worst nightmare.

Buzz drove in and screeched to a stop in the same yellow Cadillac convertible. But the sander humming loudly prevented Ed from hearing Buzz's car pulling in the driveway.

Denny, ever vigilant, barked a couple of times when the Cadillac stopped, but, because of the sander, Ed didn't hear him either.

Denny always greeted everyone who showed up at the house. He jumped up on the side of the Cadillac and draped his big paws over the window opening.

"Get down you mangy mut," Buzz hollered.

Denny dropped his head and trotted away.

Raymond had sat frozen in the swing, taking it all in.

Buzz got out of the car and checked the door of his vintage Cadillac. Finding a tiny scratch near the window, he turned around, stooped down, and called Denny. Always ready to be petted, the obedient dog went to Buzz who stood up and kicked Denny in the side. The dog yelped and ran past Raymond and out of sight around the house.

Meanwhile, Ed was still sanding on the wooden foot and was oblivious at anything going on outside.

Buzz walked over to Raymond, still frozen in the swing.

"Who are you, boy?"

"Raymond. I be a friend of William's."

"Where is Mr. Anderson?"

"He's in the barn fixing William's special feet."

That got Buzz's attention. "What in the hell are special feet?"

Raymond just sat frozen.

"Answer me, boy," said Buzz, taking a step toward Raymond.

With that, Raymond jumped out of the swing and ran out of sight.

Buzz started toward the barn shop to confront Ed but decided to take a peek in the window first when his curiosity started getting the best of him. So he stealthily grabbed an empty crate that someone had left outside and drug it below the window.

Buzz stepped up on the crate and peeking in the window, had a perfect view of William sitting in the chair. His little hooves were sticking straight out as Ed stood nearby sanding a wooden foot.

Buzz couldn't believe his eyes, so he stepped down, but then, a few seconds later, he stepped back up for a second look.

Well, I'll be damned. A goat boy, Buzz thought with amazement.

He jumped down and returned quickly back to his Cadillac and eased quietly out of the driveway. Then he hollered with excitement as he hit the highway and sped away. "Won't be long now! I just discovered a gold mine!"

*****

Ed finished sanding the wooden feet, turned off the sander, then attached them back onto William's hooves with the screws.

"Okay, son. See if you can pull your boots on now."

William pulled both boots on over his wooden feet with ease.

“It’s easy now, Dad. You fixed ’em good. Can I go play with Raymond now?”

“Yes, you can. You’ve been very patient with me again.”

“I was a good patient, wasn’t I, Dad?”

“Yes, you were, William,” Ed said, laughing.

As Ed and William left the barn, they were met by a frantic Raymond. He was talking so fast that Ed couldn’t understand a word he was saying. It took Ed a while to calm him down.

“Now slow down, Raymond. Take your time and tell me what happened.”

“There be a real mean man here just a bit ago. He kicked Denny hard and I thought he was gonna get me, too, but I run away.”

It took Ed a few minutes to get the complete story but he knew that the mean man had to be his stepbrother Buzz, especially when Raymond said the man was in a “big yaller car.”

What Ed couldn’t understand was whether Raymond had told Buzz he (Ed) and William were in the shop. And if he had told him, why would Buzz leave unless, Ed thought, *Oh my God! I hope he didn't see anything.*

But there was no reason to fret over it. If Buzz did see anything, there was nothing anyone could do about it.

So Ed turned his attention to his best canine friend, who had just wandered up to them.

He bent down and felt around Denny's body. The dog yelped when Ed touched a sensitive area on his chest but he couldn't feel any broken ribs.

Ed said, "I think he has a cracked rib but he'll be okay. If he's not better in a few days, we can take him to the vet. We just need to be real gentle with him. No roughhousing, boys."

*****

Later in the day, to take his mind off possible pending problems, Ed made good progress in raking more hay, feeding the livestock, and repairing some furniture in his home. Satisfied with his work, he poured himself a glass of iced tea, sat in his rocking chair on the front porch, and looked in the distance at the lake. He never tired of staring in awe at spectacular Watauga Lake. *Wouldn't it be nice,* he thought, *to just kick back on one of those big houseboats and fish from sunup to sundown?*

It had turned out to be a beautiful, blue-sky day with a warm wind—ideal for fishing, hiking, canoeing, or even scrounging around in the woods for ginseng.

But for whatever reason, for Ed Anderson, there never seemed to be much time for fun.

"Because a farmer's work is never done," he reminded himself, parroting what he'd heard his parents say a thousand times.

Just then, his phone rang.

As Ed had expected, it was Buzz.

"I want what I deserve, Ed, and I want it now," he demanded.

"Because you, big brother, are sittin' on a gold mine. I saw that little goat boy you're raisin' and he should be worth a fortune."

"I don't know what you thought you saw, Buzz, but who would believe you anyway? People would just think you're crazy."

"Are you willing to chance that, big brother? I'm sure I can convince people enough to investigate. Which would make little goat boy's life hell. It would be much easier to give me what I want and make this all go away."

Ed said nothing for a minute. Unfortunately, Ed knew, Buzz had the upper hand.

As hard as it was, he asked Buzz what exactly he wanted.

"Let's put it this way, big brother. I been checkin' real estate around here and forty acres as close to the lake as you are goes for over two-hundred thousand dollars. But I ain't gonna' nickel and dime you for the rest of your life. Besides that, I know you got money in the bank. We can make a one-time deal and I'm out of your life for good. I want fifty thousand dollars in cash. As in God We Trust. I'll call you tomorrow and tell you where to bring it.

"Put the money in a small travel bag and have it ready or the goat boy becomes the talk-of-the town. Or, if you want, you can just bring me the little goat boy."

"You're a low life scum bag, Buzz! But I'll give you the money. Don't call me till Friday. I need time to get the cash."

The following day Ed went to the bank and made arrangements to transfer money from several savings accounts so he could draw out fifty thousand dollars in cash. People at the bank were a bit skeptical but he explained that it was for a land purchase and the seller insisted on cash.

Friday came and Buzz called about 10 a.m. He told Ed to bring the bag of money to the Blue Circle Drive-in fast-food restaurant where he would be waiting in his Cadillac. He was to toss the bag inside Buzz' s car.

When Ed did what he was instructed to do, Buzz smirked as he unzipped the bag and glanced inside at the rolls of big bills.

"Now this is what I call some real brotherly love," Buzz said.

"Come back here again and I'll kill you. I won't hesitate."

"Not a very nice way to talk to your own brother, Ed. My goodness! You'd be better off practicin' what they preach in that church you've been goin' to."

"You're no brother to me and never will be," Ed snapped.

Buzz just smirked and sped away.

CHAPTER 11

Festive Occasion

Come fall, the mountains of East Tennessee burst with dazzling colors.

The forests were a glorious palette of deep reds, golds, burnt oranges, and greens.

Brown leaves, crunchy to the feet when you strolled through them, covered the forest floor.

And the air, now gradually getting cooler, felt crisp and clean.

Framing Watauga Lake, the thickly wooded mountains of the Cherokee National Forest seemed especially magical this time of year. Not only were they beautiful and inspiring for nature lovers. They were also the federally protected home of bald eagles, hawks, bears, white-tailed deer, bobcats, wild turkeys, and a wide range of other wildlife.

This was also the season for catching up on all the chores that Ed Anderson and his close friend John Washington had not gotten around to during the summer.

That being the case, John had decided to make sure the roof over his head would hold up even in the hardest storm. So, because it was a bright sunny day—ideal for getting outside work accomplished—the big Black man was hard at it, nailing down a piece of tin on the roof of the old log house where he and his son Raymond lived.

"House is startin' to look good again, John!" Ed yelled from the window of his pickup truck. "It's been a while since I've been on this part of the property."

"Thanks, Mr. Ed," John said, "and you know you always be welcome to drop in hea' anytime you want to. I just hope the good Lord won't mind me workin' on Sunday. I aim to fix this roof befo' the snows come."

"That reminds me, big fella. Next Thursday is Thanksgiving. Do you and Raymond have any plans?"

"No Sir, Mr. Ed. Me and my boy just gonna have our Thanksgiving here."

Ed replied: "Then you have it with us. Madge will be cookin' a feast, and no need for y'all to bring anything."

"That's real nice, Mr. Ed, but—"

"No buts, John. You're having Thanksgiving dinner with us."

*****

Light snow fell on the big holiday as John, in clean overalls and a plaid shirt, lugged an armload of split wood through the back door of Ed's house. With him was his son Raymond, who, for this special occasion, (with a little help from his dad,) had combed his hair and put on his Sunday best.

John carried the wood to the living room and laid it on the large hearth.

A fire crackled in the big stone fireplace as Madge, taking rolls from the oven, shouted a "Happy Thanksgiving" greeting to John and his son Raymond.

"Y'all sure look nice," she said, straightening her apron. "Now wash up, fellows. We're puttin' it on the table. And Ed, I'll need your help. Many hands make light work."

After William and Raymond had, at the same time, washed their hands in the bathroom, John followed their example and washed his. Then he took the crumpled towel the boys had used and dried off—very carefully hanging the towel on the towel rack so that it was straight.

In the dining room, he and Ed sat at each end of the big walnut table, which Madge had decorated with red candles, pinecones, and a white tablecloth. The boys sat on one side and Madge on the other.

"Our hands are clean, Miss Madge," William said. "And WOW! Look at our turkey, Raymond. She sure is lookin' like a juicy bird!"

Everyone at the table heartily agreed that they might be having the best Thanksgiving feast in Laketon.

Madge had spared nothing in preparing their meal—which included giblet gravy, mashed potatoes, cranberry sauce, dressing, apple raisin salad, turkey, and fresh hot rolls. For drinks, everyone had either water, apple cider, or tea.

William asked: "Dad, can me and Raymond watch football after we eat? We want ta' play football in high school."

"And college, too," added Raymond.

When Ed allowed that they could all watch it after eating such a delicious grand meal, Madge asked William if he'd like to say the blessing.

"Yes Ma'am."

So, everyone held hands and closed their eyes as William, searching for words, began:

"Dear Lord, let us be thankful for this food we are about to____."

William stumbled and stammered trying to find the right word.

Ed, helping him, said, "It's a word used in football a lot, William."

"A______" (still at a loss for the right word).

"I know!" Raymond offered.

"Okay. Let's let Raymond say the blessing," Ed said.

"Dear Lord, let us be thankful for this food we are about to TACKLE."

Which elicited laughter from Ed, John, and Madge and even William and an awe-shucks look from Raymond.

When Raymond hit his head with his hand, Madge corrected them, "RECEIVE, you silly boys."

With that, Ed carved up the big turkey, dishes were passed around, and everyone served themselves.

“This be the most happiest, blessed Thanksgivin’ I ever been a part of,” said John. “Me an’ Raymond so glad we be with y’all.”

CHAPTER 12

Close Call On The Gridiron

(Years Later)

The two boys' love for football remained strong as they grew older, and now, William, 17, stood 6 feet tall and was a muscular 175 pounds. Handsome, with long blond hair, Ed's son cut quite a figure in his football uniform.

Likewise, William's best friend Raymond had earned the name "Stringbean" because at 6 feet, 6 inches, 190 pounds and with short, cropped hair, he was the fastest member of the Laketon High School Panthers football team.

"We'll beat 'em tomorrow night," Raymond assured William as the two of them finished practice for the upcoming game against Cloudland.

"Lookin' good, fellows!" their coach yelled to his team as they began taking off their pads and helmets and started exiting the practice field. "But listen up. Tomorrow's an important game for two reasons. For one, we haven't lost to Cloudland in six years. And another thing—there'll be some scouts here tomorrow night from ETSU. So if you're lookin' for a scholarship, I suggest you give it all you got!"

The players, exhausted from the final pregame practice, responded with okays and headed to the locker room.

William, walking alongside Raymond, said, "You've been sayin' you wanted to go to ETSU. Tomorrow night, you get a chance to show 'em what you got."

"Whaddya think, William? Have I got a shot at it?"

"You kiddin'? You're a shoe-in, Raymond. You're the best receiver to come out of Laketon in years."

Raymond wasn't convinced. "But I need you, William. We work good together. Wouldn't be nothin' without you throwin' the ball."

"Don't kid yourself, Raymond," William said. "I might be a good high school player, but I'm never gonna' get picked by a college coach. You know it. And I'm okay with that cause I wanna do something else."

"Yeah, I know. You want to be a doctor, don't you?" Raymond said. "And you'll be a good one, William. That I know for sure."

As the two boys passed a group of cheerleaders who themselves had been practicing for the upcoming big game, one of the young women, a pompom dangling from her right hand, ran up to Raymond.

She was Gwen, a light-skinned 16-year-old pretty Black girl with long dark braids.

"I've been watchin' you, Raymond, and I know you're gonna take me out after the game tomorrow night. Now ain't that right," she said teasingly.

Raymond just blushed and nodded slightly.

Then she turned to William, who was wiping dirt and sweat off his brow with his arm.

"And you, William. Why don't you get a date and go to the dance with us after the game?'

"I'll see," he grunted.

*****

On game night, with the scoreboard in the fourth quarter showing 'Home—17 Cloudland—21' the Laketon Panthers had possession on Cloudland's 24-yard line with 30 seconds left on the clock.

Ed, Madge, John, and Doc Benson watched intently as the center snapped the football to William.

Raymond, meanwhile, had crossed the goal line and jumped high to get in the clear. He waved his arms frantically, trying to catch his quarterback (William's) attention.

Escaping one tackler and then two more who thought they had him in their grasps, William located Raymond and hit him with a perfect pass.

As his best friend grabbed the pass, the clock ran out and the crowd roared.

John, Ed, Madge and Doc Benson cheered loudly and high-fived each other.

And the college scout from ETSU was overheard saying, "We need Raymond Washington."

But then came a troubling announcement on the P.A. system.

"We have a man down, ladies and gentlemen! It's number 28, the Panthers' quarterback—William Anderson. He's not moving. Please pray for William."

An eerie, chilling silence immediately came over the crowd, as first responders hurried out onto the field. Paramedics immediately placed William on a stretcher and were in the process of loading him into an ambulance. But Doc Benson and Ed got there just in the nick of time.

“We don’t want ’em taking William to the hospital or all hell will break loose,” Doc warned Ed. “Let’s make sure the rescue squad takes him to my clinic.”

Agreeing with Doc, Ed bent down, gripped his son’s right hand, and asked him if he was okay.

“I’m okay, Dad, but this time it really hurt bad,” William said between sobs.

“Hang in there, buddy,” Raymond said. “You’re gonna’ be okay.”

Doc and Ed lifted William up and began moving him so that he didn’t have to put any weight on his feet.

As he was placed in the ambulance, he noticed the final outcome of the game on the stadium scoreboard: Home—24 Cloudland—21.

William flashed a big smile and a thumbs-up to Raymond and the rest of his teammates who had gathered around to wish him well.

His coach stuck his head in the ambulance and told William he was being awarded the game ball.

"And Doc," the coach said, "will you let me know soon as you find out what the prognosis is? Ed, you be sure to tell William he won this game—with Raymond's help."

"I've never seen a bone injury like that," one of paramedics muttered as the ambulance left. "Why, his left foot was turned completely around. He'll be lucky if he ever walks again."

Gwen, noticing Raymond had his head hung low, approached him and said that if he didn't want to go to the dance that night, she understood.

"But are you okay?" she asked.

"Yeah—and I ain't goin' nowhere tonight. I'm just worried about my best friend William."

CHAPTER 13

Smitten

Thanks to Doc Benson and lots of physical therapy, William made good progress with his injury.

So good that even with a cast covering his left foot and extending to his knee, he got around fairly well on crutches.

Not that any of the three-day-a-week rehab was easy, but he had excellent physical therapists who encouraged him to stay with a strict schedule of stretching exercises.

They had never actually laid eyes on the damaged goat foot inside his cast. Only Doc Benson and Ed had done that. And they kept reminding William that no one else, under any circumstance, was to see his bare feet.

They assured William that those who truly loved him paid no mind to why his feet were so different.

"You were made that way, Son, and that's all there is to it," Ed had said over and over. "And only the Good Lord knows why, but I'm sure He's got his reasons."

His dad's words echoed through his mind as one day on his crutches, William slowly climbed the steep rocky hill behind where they lived. A cool mountain breeze felt good as he plopped down on a stump near several pet and animal markers under a sprawling pine tree.

Etched in one of the wooden markers was "DENNY—Always In Our Hearts"

William bowed his head and prayed that the beloved Denny was in dog heaven.

Then he made his way back down the hill. Along the way, he encountered his dad's whirligig. He stopped for a few minutes to watch the little weathered wooden man dancing in the wind. The man needed a new coat of paint and William reminded himself to do that within the next few days.

"You gettin' around pretty good on those crutches," his dad said as his son entered the house. "Where you been?"

"Up to our little cemetery on the hill. I sure miss old Denny, Dad. I think we oughta' get another dog."

Ed was still emotional about losing his best friend, "Maybe someday, son. I need to get over Denny first."

Someone knocked on the front door and it turned out to be none other than Ann Smith with her daughter Leigh, 18. She was average height and build with shoulder length auburn hair and blue eyes.

William couldn't take his eyes off her. He was immediately smitten.

Dang, she's a nice-lookin' gal, he thought.

"Ann Smith!" Ed said loudly. "Come on in. And who's that you've got with you?'

"You remembered me," she said, cracking a smile.

"Of course I remembered you!" Ed hugged her and then turned to the young pretty woman.

"This is my daughter Leigh. I should have called you, Ed, but Leigh wanted to come to Johnson City and check out ETSU and tour the campus. We did that yesterday."

"No need to apologize at all, Ann. You know you and your daughter are always welcome here. Come sit with us."

As they sat down in the living room—Ann next to Ed, and her attractive daughter in the chair beside William—Ann began explaining to Leigh how they were connected.

"I wanted to show her how beautiful the area is here around the lake while we were so close," Ann said. "I told Leigh all these mountains surrounding the lake were part of the Cherokee National Forest. She was amazed that white men have probably never set foot in some of the woods in these mountains around here. Then I got this sudden urge to come by your house."

"So glad you did, Ann, and Leigh, it's very nice to meet you."

Ed introduced his son William to both. But the young man couldn't seem to take his eyes off Leigh long enough to meet her mother. He also seemed to have a tough time speaking.

But then, when he finally found his voice, he invited Leigh to go to the barn with him to see the baby goats.

"Can you do that on your crutches, William?" Ann asked.

Ed assured her he could. "You'd never know he had a broken ankle."

When the two young people got up to leave, Ann asked her daughter not to stay too long "Cause we gotta' get on the road soon."

*****

When they were alone, Ed asked Ann if her daughter knew about her life in Laketon.

"She knows everything, Ed. We have no secrets. And I married a wonderful man when Leigh was 3. He's taken very good care of us. My daughter loves him dearly. But having said that, she still occasionally asks about her biological father."

Ed said that was only natural. "Just tell her the truth, Ann. He was abusive and wild and reckless and took advantage of everybody. I sure as heck saw more of that on his last visit here."

She asked him if he came back often.

"Only once so far—about five years after you left. Good riddance to him."

*****

Meanwhile, in the barn, Leigh held a baby goat, while two others jumped around the barn lot.

The little brown and white goat made eye contact with her, as goats often do with humans, and didn't look away. So, Leigh kissed the animal on the nose.

All the while, William was transfixed on Leigh.

"They're all so cute. I love their long soft ears," she said.

"That's what sets them apart from other goats," William said. "These goats are Nubians. Some people say they're smarter than dogs and even love people more than dogs do. And I'm startin' to agree with that. A baby goat is closer to being human than just about anything else in the animal kingdom."

"They sure are affectionate," she beamed.

From the house, Ann glanced out the window toward the barn.

"I'm so glad Leigh will have a friend at college. I like William."

"She'll have many," Ed said reassuringly. "Because William has lots of friends and several are going to ETSU. I don't know if you ever met John Anderson, the Black man?"

When Ann said she wasn't sure, Ed explained that John worked and lived here on his (Ed's) property, and that he had a son Raymond, the same age as William, who happened to be his son's best friend.

"And Raymond just got a football scholarship to ETSU," Ed said. "He and William will look after Leigh at the university. They'll take good care of her."

CHAPTER 14

Campus Life

During registration for classes at ETSU, William made sure he accompanied Leigh every step of the way. If she signed up for a certain section of history or biology or government or whatever the class might be, he signed up for that same course and section.

Same with clubs or organizations on campus.

When Leigh joined the Fellowship of Christian Athletes (because she played volleyball at ETSU), so did William. Because he had been a star quarterback in high school, he aspired, one day, to be on the cross-country team at ETSU.

And when she decided to become a member of the First Christian Church of Johnson City, William joined that same church with her.

Anything, anytime, just to be with Leigh.

And when they weren't in class or studying, they were dating—whether that meant going to a movie, catching a bite to eat at an area restaurant, going for long walks in the city's beautiful parks, or just hanging out together with friends.

That's the way their relationship started and continued, pretty much, for the first two years of their time at the university.

And then, at the beginning of year three, they became much more serious—to the point that they couldn't stand to be apart which was difficult, because Leigh lived in a closely monitored all-female dorm where men were only allowed for brief visits.

And William commuted to campus from home in Laketon.

Still, however, they found a way to stay closely together—even if it meant skirting some of the overnight visitation rules at Leigh's dorm.

*****

On one occasion, for example, with her roommate being out of town, Leigh invited William to spend the night with her.

She didn't have to ask him twice.

And next thing you knew, the two of them were in bed in Leigh's room soon after dinner.

After enjoying each other immensely, the two young people caught their breath, looked into each other's eyes and sensuously explored each other's mouth with their tongues.

"Mom said you would take good care of me, but wow! Was that ever an understatement," Leigh, her right hand on his bare chest, said with a giggle.

"I'd do anything for you, Leigh. You know that," said William, his western style boots sticking out from under a sheet at the end of her dorm room bed.

"Well, then, I have to ask you a question, William, and I want a straight answer."

He interrupted her right there.

"If you're going to ask me why I never take my boots off, don't. You just have to accept that they will never come off. We've been over this before."

Leigh stared at him intensely.

"I know, William, but it doesn't make any sense. I don't care if you have some kind of deformity. All I know is I love you, and I'll always love you and nothing'll ever change that.

"Now take those damn boots off!" she demanded.

Reminding her that she had broken a promise she had made to him early in their relationship, William jumped out of bed in his shorts, pulled his loose-fitting jeans over his boots, and put on a tee shirt and jacket. Then he stormed out the door.

"Maybe you shouldn't come back," Leigh screamed as William, ignoring wolf whistles made by girls, hurried down the hall and out the exit into the dark.

*****

A few days later, desperately missing each other, William asked Leigh to accompany him on a visit to Mikey's, a local hangout for college students.

She accepted and they were soon sitting together at a table in the combination restaurant/bar, enjoying one of Mikey's flame grilled burgers.

Before dessert, Leigh pulled William out onto the dance floor, and they stared dreamily into one another's eyes as they slow danced to the song played from an old-fashioned jukebox— "You Are So Beautiful."

"I'm sorry, Leigh," William whispered to her.

Instead of responding, she held him more tightly, their bodies practically becoming one on the intimate, dimly lit dance floor.

"Hey buddy," a big hulking man shouted from the bar. "Mind if I cut in and have a dance with that sweet gal in your arms?"

He was Biff Barrett, a mainstay of the ETSU football team. He stood 6 feet, 4 inches, had thick arms, a barrel chest, and weighed about 250 pounds.

And that night, he was obnoxious and feeling his oats, having downed half a dozen cold beers.

"Check out the sweet thing in that guy's arms," Biff yelled to his friends.

Then the big imposing football player got down off the stool and grabbed Leigh by the wrist as she and William attempted to walk away from him.

Startled, she looked at Biff and tried to pull away.

"I would LOVE to dance with you, pretty lady," he said.

"No thank you. Now could you please let me go?"

This sparked William to speak up. "She's with me," he said, trying to control his anger and fear.

"Really? Well, I'm sure you won't mind if I dance with her, will you, little man?"

"I think I heard her say no," William said.

Biff moved closer to William and got in his face.

"You don't know who I am, do you?"

"You're Biff Barrett, offensive lineman for the Buccaneers."

"Good for you, whatever your name is," Biff said. "So, I'm gonna' dance with this lady. Then she's yours for the rest of the night."

Leigh, fear in her voice, said, "I'll dance with him, William. Then we can go."

This elicited Mikey, the gray-templed 50ish bar owner, to intervene and try to diffuse the situation.

"Biff, if you don't leave these people alone right now, I'll have to ask you to leave," he said sternly.

But Biff didn't budge.

"This here gal wants to dance with me, Mikey, and I aim ta please her. There's no problem here. Ain't that right, boy?" Biff said. He was nose to nose with William.

William pushed Biff out of his face and tried to reason with him.

"She doesn't really want to dance with you, Biff. She's just afraid for me."

"And she should be!" Biff declared. "And don't put your damn hands on me!"

Mikey again tried to defuse things.

"Come on, Biff. Now that's enough!" he said.

William said, "I'm sorry, Biff, but you had your face right in mine and your breath is bad."

Biff got even more angry: "Now this smart ass is insulting me."

Mikey pulled him by the arm and implored the big hunk of a man to sit down.

"Not till this asshole apologizes!" Biff demanded.

"I'm sorry you have bad breath," William said.

"I still think you're a smart ass," said Biff, now even angrier.

Suddenly, he took William by surprise, grabbing his shoulders and head butting him. They bumped heads so violently that the sound of their painful moans could be heard over the loud music.

Biff, who seemed to get the worst of the collision, stood straight up, his eyes frozen in a glare. Then he fell straight back, hitting the floor with such force that patrons sitting at tables across the room felt it. He was out cold.

William, slightly dazed, touched his own forehead and noticed a touch of blood on his hand.

Mikey, also seeing the blood, pulled a bar towel out of his back pocket and patted William on his head.

When he asked William if he was okay, William gave him a thumbs up. Then Mikey knelt down and patted Biff on his face, trying to bring him around.

"Maybe you folks better leave before this gorilla comes to," he said.

William nodded his agreement and said he needed to pay his tab.

"It's on the house," Mikey, sweat rolling off his forehead, said. "Now all of you get outta here. It was worth it. I'll have some choice words to say to Biff's head coach tomorrow morning."

CHAPTER 15

True Confession

Monday morning the next day, Leigh rose early so she could be on time to her class at 8. She brushed her hair, put on her makeup, got dressed, made herself a cup of hot coffee, a bagel with creamed cheese, and a blueberry pop tart (her sweet treat for the day).

She had gathered her backpack, crammed with pens, pencils, books, and a notepad and was on her way to her dorm room door when someone knocked.

It was William.

"Come on in but don't make me late for class," she said.

He promised her he wouldn't be long.

"That's what you always say," she said with a smile. She sat on the bed. "But that's my William."

"First of all, I'm sorry I stormed out on you the other day," he said. "You deserve better, but I need you to understand____"

Leigh interrupted him and took him by the hand.

"Before you start, may I say something? I know when our relationship first started, I agreed to never ask you to take your boots off. To never question you about something that you're very sensitive about. I thought, okay, that's no big deal. But William, I didn't know then that you would become the love of my life—the person I intend to spend the rest of my life with. You just have to trust me with whatever you're keeping to yourself. I promise, never, ever to hurt you."

William said he did trust her but added that he believed she would be so shocked that she'd never again have anything to do with him.

"Because I'm not sure you could handle what you'd find out about me, Leigh."

"Just let me be the judge of that," she said, squeezing his hands tightly in her own.

"Leigh, it'll be a big shock, and if it ever gets out, my life would never be normal. And I have dreams—things I want to accomplish and things I want to experience."

He choked up as he continued.

"And I want, more than anything else in the world to experience them with you. So, it'll have to be a lifelong commitment that you'll never reveal what

I'm about to show you. You sure you can handle that?"

Leigh said nothing for a few seconds, then asked him, "Are you an alien, William?"

When he said he wasn't, she responded, "I don't care if you have duck feet, William, because I love you and I can handle anything you show me."

William sat down in a chair close to the bed.

"Close your eyes, Leigh, and give me your solemn promise that what you're about to learn is not shared with anyone else for as long as you live. You have to promise."

"I promise," she said, "but I'll have to admit, you've got me really curious."

With her eyes still shut, William pulled his chair close to the bed and took a Swiss army knife out of his pocket. Then he sat back and pulled off one of his western style boots exposing his wooden foot.

"You can open your eyes now, Leigh."

Which she did. She watched as he folded out the Phillips screwdriver on the knife and backed out the screws on each side of the wooden foot. Then he pulled out his hoof.

Leigh covered her eyes at first but then put her hands down and began crying.

"I've never seen anything like this in my life," she said between sobs, "but it only makes me love you more."

"I'm sorry. I've already made you late for class," William said.

"Class!" she said. "Who cares about class today? I'm not going. But I do want you to explain to me what I'm looking at." She couldn't take her eyes off his hoof.

William said he'd try and then asked her if she'd ever heard about in-vitro fertilization.

"Sure," she said. "It's when an egg is fertilized in a test tube because some women can't get pregnant the normal way. Then they put the fertilized egg in her uterus where it grows to full term. Right?"

"Close enough," he said. "What if a fertilized egg was put in a uterus that wasn't human?"

"Is THAT what happened?" she asked incredulously.

"That's part of it. I believe you've met Dad's good friend, Doc Benson?"

When she said she had, William told her that Doc was one of four people—Dad, Doc, Madge, and himself—who knew what he was about to reveal to her.

"This is what Doc thinks might have happened," William said. "A fertilized human egg was placed in a nanny goat's uterus, and there might have been male goat sperm present at the time. Or she could have gotten with one of Dad's male goats at our farm after Dad got her.

"Regardless, I'm the result," William added. "I was born in the barn at the farm and Dad—God bless him—chose to raise me as a normal child. I'm the result of a procedure gone wrong by a geneticist who was experimenting at home with animals. He died of a heart attack and so we don't know exactly what happened. But that's how Dad ended up with the nanny goat and ultimately with me."

Leigh, silent at first, swallowed hard and then spoke: "I see. Is it only your feet that are different?"

"Doc says the only other thing is my skull. It's a little thicker than normal. That's it."

"So, you're hardheaded?" she said with a laugh.

"You might say that," he said. "Biff knows that now."

When she didn't say anything for a few seconds, William got up from the chair, kissed her on the cheek, and sat back down. Then he slipped his hoof back into the wood foot and tightened the screws holding his foot straight and pulled his boot on. Then he rose and started toward the door.

"Where are you going?" Leigh asked.

"Well, this is a lot to digest, Leigh, and if you want me to walk out that door and out of your life, I totally understand. But if you want me to stay, I'll love you till the day I die."

"Sit down, William," Leigh said softly.

William did as he was told.

Leigh slid off the bed and got on her knees in front of him. Taking his right ankle in her hand, she pulled it up and slipped off his boot.

Holding William's wooden foot against her cheek, she declared,

"You're not going anywhere, and neither am I! Because I love you, William Anderson, and I always will."

CHAPTER 16

Special Announcement

(One Year Later)

Spring and summer went by quickly, with Leigh and William escaping on several weekends to their favorite campground at Cades Cove in the Smoky Mountains National Park. They liked tent camping, hiking, birdwatching and wading in the cool mountain streams of the Smokies.

But even on the weekends, they had their books and class notes with them so that they could keep pace with their summer courses at ETSU. And because those courses met only once or twice a week, the young couple still had plenty of time for fun escapes from their small apartment they now shared near the campus.

Before long, the seasons changed. The air got much cooler and crisper, leaves fell from trees, and the pungent smells of autumn filled the senses.

And then, on Thanksgiving Day, Leigh and William found themselves back at the farm (where William was born) in Laketon. They had been invited to come eat turkey and all the trimmings with Ed and Madge.

As they stepped up onto the back porch of Ed's house, William noticed the little wood man dancing in the wind.

"Some things never change," he said. "Because I've been watching that little guy dance for all my life, it seems."

Then, with Leigh's help, he scooped up an armful of firewood, and they entered through the back door.

The sweet smells coming from the kitchen—from pecan and pumpkin pies, turkey, dressing, and freshly baked bread— made their mouths water.

Ed had just taken a turkey from the oven as Madge began spreading butter on a pan of hot rolls.

"Wash up, William," she said. "It's going on the table."

"Man, that turkey smells good, Dad," he said. "And did you know that the little man is dancing? Maybe it's going to snow."

Ed, after hugging Leigh, said, "It could happen, son. It's cold enough."

William, agreeing, took the firewood to the living room and laid it on the hearth.

Meanwhile, Leigh—always fond of animals—had begun petting a little yellow lab puppy.

"What's little Winston up to," William asked Leigh.

Leigh said the adorable dog kept falling asleep, even though he wanted to play. But he was too worn out.

"Isn't he precious," she said. "But who named him Winston?"

William said his dad had, but he wasn't sure why.

Leigh then told William that he had made the right choice in getting the puppy for his dad. Not that any animal could ever replace Denny, she said, but a man who had been through as much as Ed needed a dog—plain and simple.

"Come and eat," Madge commanded them. "It's on the table."

William quickly hurried to wash his hands as the others seated themselves for the holiday feast.

When he got back to the table, Madge asked him to say the blessing.

"Thank you, Lord, for this wonderful day when we can all be together," he said, "and thank you for this food we are about to tackle."

Madge, Ed, and William laughed while Leigh just smiled.

Then Madge filled her in on how the words of William's prayer had come to be.

"And William's been saying the same blessing ever since," she said.

Ed, serving himself a big scoop of mashed potatoes, asked his son how Raymond was doing.

"Pretty good, Dad. He's really made a name for himself on the Bucs football team, and I have a feeling he might one day play in the NFL."

"Well, now wouldn't that be something!" Ed beamed. "Be sure to give him our best. And what ever happened to that cute little girl he was seeing?" he asked. "What was her name?"

"Gwen and she and Raymond're extremely close. The four of us get together a lot," said Leigh.

"Well, maybe for the next big occasion, you could invite them to come eat with us," Madge said.

“Dad, how is John, Raymond’s dad doing?”

“John is doing fine, William. He went to visit his brother and his family in Knoxville for Thanksgiving. If he hadn’t, he’d be here at the table with us.”

Madge turned to Leigh and told her how happy she was that she was joining them for Thanksgiving.

“I just hope your family was okay with it, dear.”

“They were fine with it, Ma’am,” Leigh said. “William and I are going to spend Christmas with them.”

“That’s good, and Leigh, just call me Madge.”

“Dad, Leigh asks me why you named your new pup Winston.”

William looked toward his dad for an answer.

“Well, there’s a story there if you all want to hear it.” Ed put his fork down.

“As long as it’s over before dessert,” Madge said.

“Well, as most of you don’t know, my father, Omar Anderson, was born in the United Kingdom in a small village called Lavenham. He came with his parents to the U.S as a small child. Dad, knowing he was from the U.K, always admired Winston Churchill, the prime minister. That's where my dad's Winston got his name.

"But there's more to the story."

"Okay, go ahead and finish it," said Madge with a smile.

"Dad was a small child when they came to the U.S. and settled on this land. They farmed it and this is where Dad grew up. Anyway, to make a long story short, when Dad was in his mid-80s probably two or three years after Mom had passed, a little throw away stray pup wandered onto the farm. Now my father had never owned a dog or any kind of pet in his life.

"His parents said they were not practical. The only reason they kept goats is because they drank the milk and made goat cheese.

"Why feed something that does nothing for you?" they often said.

Anyway, Dad started feeding the little starving pup and before you knew it, he had named him Winston and the dog had moved into the house.

“Dad loved little Winston who stuck to him like beggar lice.

“To make a long story even shorter, when Dad turned 89, he still insisted on helping on the farm and when he did, Winston was always beside him.

“I found my father dead in the barn, with a pitchfork in his hand. He was attempting to clean out one of the stalls where the baby goats slept at night.

“Little Winston was lying beside him,” Ed said as he choked back tears.

“We buried Dad in that little cemetery down by the lake, beside Mom, and Winston was there during the burial.

“When I couldn’t find Winston that night to feed him, I looked all over the farm. Then out of desperation, I went down to the cemetery, and he was there lying on Dad’s grave.

“I took him home and fed him and when I let him out, he went back to the grave site. That went on for several days until I found the little fellow dead curled up on Dad’s grave.

“That night after dark, I went back down to the cemetery and buried little Winston a few feet down, right over Dad.

"So, I named my little Winston in honor of my dad's little Winston."

"What a sad story," said Leigh, tears running down her cheeks.

"Well, it is, and it isn't," said Ed.

Madge, also teary eyed, asked him to explain.

"It's sad because Winston died, but it isn't because I like to believe that Dad, Mom, and little Winston are all together now in heaven enjoying each other."

"So, you believe dogs go to heaven, too," Leigh asked.

Ed said that several verses in the Bible suggested that. "In Ecclesiastes 3:18-21 it says, "All flesh shall see the salvation of God."

"Your dad is really smart, isn't he, William?" asked Leigh.

"Well, like he always tells me, I'll tell you. He's smarter than the average bear."

Everyone patted their eyes dry and laughed.

Meanwhile, Winston had been under and around the table whimpering and even standing up on his hind legs with his tongue hanging out. When he barked suddenly and loudly, Ed took a small piece of turkey and handed it to the pup, who devoured it in seconds.

Madge said, "I see little Winston is taking up where Denny left off."

Ed replied, "Just the way I like it. He reminds me of him every day. But you know what? There'll never be another Denny. He filled all our souls with love. Now it's Winston's turn."

William, looking nervous and unsure of himself, stood up and said he had an announcement to make. "Dad's story will be hard to follow but I'll try."

Leigh smiled as he at first cleared his throat and wiped his mouth with the Thanksgiving-themed cloth napkin that Madge had specially ordered.

Everyone put their eating utensils down and stared at William, who didn't say anything until the room was completely silent.

"What I want to tell you is that Leigh and I are engaged and plan to get married right after we graduate this spring," he said.

Madge couldn't contain her joy. "That's absolutely wonderful!" Then she rushed up and hugged both Leigh and William.

Ed, on the other hand, seemed a bit reserved.

"We all love you, Leigh, but what do you know about my son?" he asked softly.

Leigh, taking William's hand, said she knew William to be a sweet, caring, honest man. "And he's funny and handsome, I might add, and he loves me very much."

Ed still was reserved, and William sensed it.

"She knows everything, Dad."

"Then you've sold me, Leigh," Ed said. "You both have my blessings."

Madge proposed a toast, and they all put their glasses together.

"May I?" Ed asked.

"It's your house and you surely may," Madge said.

"Then may you bring each other as much joy and happiness as you have brought us," he said as they clinked their glasses together.

Outside the huge picture window, framed with blue calico pullback curtains, William noticed white stuff was falling from the sky.

Big, wet snowflakes were hitting the ground but melting.

Everyone, especially Ed, would have loved for the first snow of winter—on Thanksgiving Day—to stick.

But no matter. It had still been a very special day.

CHAPTER 17

Bad News

(8 Months Later)

Ed, with John's steadfast help, continued grinding away at the farm. There was always something to do—whether tending to the animals, hauling and stacking hay, repairing fences, plowing the garden, or executing the seemingly endless tasks associated with owning a home.

A wedding was on the near horizon and Ed knew that there would be receptions, parties, or other special events held at his farm. So, he wanted everything to look spiffy and be in good working order as the big date got closer.

One afternoon, in the middle of helping a momma cow deliver a calf, he got so tired that he sat down in the pasture under a shade tree.

Somethin's wrong with me. I never used to run out of energy like this. And why've I been losing weight?

He thought about his late wife Daisy and how fatigued she'd gotten near the end.

But not me! No way I could be getting that death sentence. I've got to be here for William and Leigh.

Still, he figured it wouldn't hurt to pay a visit to Doc Benson. And so, the following day he found himself at the Laketon Clinic. A pretty young nurse had taken his vitals and insurance info and said the good doctor would be with him shortly.

When the respected physician entered the holding room where Ed sat, he had a grim expression. He had already run some lab tests on his old friend and had developed a prognosis.

Ed intuited—from the doctor's nonverbals—it was not promising.

"Just spit it out, Doc. I know it's not good."

The doctor glanced one last time at his notes and then tried, Ed knew, to maintain his composure.

"It's serious, but it's not a death certificate, Ed. People have survived pancreatic cancer. And the lab tests show you definitely have it. I'm just surprised you didn't get your butt in here earlier. Because how long have you been feelin' weak and shedding pounds?"

Ed said he'd been having stomach aches and dark urine, along with low energy for about a month.

Peggy Sue shared with him that Leigh's mom, Ann, had worked at the Laketon Grocery about 20-some-odd years ago."

Then, lowering her voice, she said, "But I heard through the grapevine she left here when she got pregnant with the girl."

"No kiddin? Who was the girl's father?"

Peggy Sue said she'd heard the dad was "some low life traveling through and the girl's mother took a likin' to him."

"Well, ain't that somethin?" Buzz said. "Doc Benson still have his little clinic here in town?"

"Yep. Sure does."

"And I guess Ann is here for the weddin'?"

"Far as I know," Peggy Sue said, "but I ain't seen her yet. She's probably over at the Methodist church. They're having a rehearsal dinner tonight. Reason I know that is I go to church there on Sundays."

"You happen to know the time of the weddin tomorrow, PP? I forgot my invitation."

"Three o'clock."

"That sounds right," Buzz said. "Well, it's been a real pleasure talkin' to you, PP. You're just a wealth of information."

"Why, thank you, Mr. Smith. But my boss says I talk too much. Do you think I talk too much?"

"Absolutely not, you just told me things I needed to know, and call me Jim."

"I will and don't you be a stranger, Jim."

As Buzz walked out the door, he crossed paths with Madge, but Madge only got a glimpse and didn't recognize him at first.

Still, however, Buzz seemed familiar.

"Who was that man, PP?"

"That was Jim Smith," she said as she put a wad of chewing gum in her mouth. "He's a friend of Ed's. Came here for the weddin'. Nice fellow."

Madge turned around and saw the yellow Cadillac backing into the street, then pulling away.

"Oh yeah," Madge said, maintaining a straight face. "Now I remember Jim Smith."

CHAPTER 18

Purloined Record

Just a few minutes past midnight at the Laketon Medical Clinic, Buzz, dressed in black and with a black bandana covering his face, got out of his Cadillac, took a crowbar from the trunk and hid it under his jacket.

After a quick look around under a pitch-black star-filled sky, he walked to the back door of the clinic. He glanced around once again, and, satisfied that he was alone, jammed the crowbar in near the lock.

He pried the door open, looked around yet again and saw not a soul, then entered.

Holding a miniature flashlight in his mouth, Buzz searched the file cabinets labeled A-B in Doc Benson's office. He flipped through all the A's and B's, then rifled through the unmarked file cabinets, breaking open the locked ones with his crowbar.

He had no luck.

So, he started opening drawers in Doc's big oak desk. Finding a locked one, he broke it open with the crowbar, and wah-lah! There, tucked inside the locked drawer was a big manila envelope labeled William Anderson.

Barely able to control his excitement, Buzz opened the envelope and pulled out a small folder of x-rays.

There, under the flashlight, it was—an x-ray of William's legs and hooves.

"Just what I needed, goat boy," Buzz muttered. "This little x-ray is gonna' change my life. And if it don't, it'll mess up your world."

*****

Earlier Madge had made an important phone call to Ed, but he didn't answer, so she spoke to an answering machine:

"Ed, this is Madge, I thought you'd want to know that Buzz is back in town, and he just talked to Peggy Sue at the grocery store. I don't know for certain, but I'd say he's up to no good. If I see him again and get a chance, I'll follow that rascal and see where he's staying."

*****

The next day, at a little white church surrounded by ancient oak trees, a big happy group of people sat at a long table in the church fellowship hall. They included Ed, Madge, Leigh, William, Doc, Ann, Raymond, Gwen, and the Rev. Hicks.

Empty plates and serving bowls, once laden with roast beef, corn on the cob, mashed potatoes, soup beans, and freshly baked bread, sat on the table.

Everyone had just finished the main course and were waiting for dessert—strawberry short cake and blackberry cobbler made by the ladies of the church.

They laughed and made merry and each of them took turns guessing where exactly (it had yet to be revealed) William and Leigh would spend their honeymoon.

Ted, Ann's husband from Georgia, asked Ed if he could have a word in private with him.

The two men walked to an unoccupied corner of the room, and Ted said: "I know it's been over 20 years, Ed, but I want to thank you for helping Ann when she was pregnant with Leigh. You can never imagine how much she needed that check you slipped into her pocket. It's just funny how things work out. Maybe your payback is having Leigh as a daughter-in-law."

"If that's the case," Ed said with a laugh, "it sounds like I came out all right on that deal."

Ted, shaking his right hand, added, "And I want you to know Ann and I are delighted with this union. We think the world of your son. He's a fine young man."

*****

Madge was true to her word about tailing Buzz if she saw him—to find out where he was staying.

It just so happened that the two people crossed one another's path, in their respective vehicles—Madge in a newer model VW and Buzz in his slick looking classic Cadillac—as the latter had stopped to fill his gas tank in Laketon.

Madge laid low as Buzz pumped his own gas and puffed on a cigarette.

Then when Buzz drove off, Madge followed him—from a distance—to the Riverview Motel in Elizabethton. She watched him exit his car and enter room 110.

Madge quickly found a pay phone and gave Ed another call.

"Hi, Madge. I just came from a meal at the church and I got the message you left on my machine."

"I saw him again, Ed, and I followed him to where he's staying'. It's a motel in Elizabethton called Riverview. He's in room 110."

"Thanks so much, sweetheart, but please stay away from Buzz. If you encounter him again, walk away. That man is dangerous and will do anything for a dollar. I love you. See you at the wedding."

Ed hung up the phone and pondered his next move. Then he took a key ring out of his pocket and unlocked his gun cabinet in the den. He took a Remington double-barreled shotgun out and sat down with the gun in his lap.

His faithful little dog Winston, always not very far away from him, seemed to sense his master was troubled. So Winston nuzzled his head on Ed's right leg, and, always up for a kind word or touch, reveled in the man petting him.

Ed looked to his right at a framed photo of Madge, then to his left at a similarly framed one of Daisy.

Somehow in all that I've been through with William and Buzz and everything else, Daisy always seems to get forgotten. But I HAVE NOT FORGOTTEN HER, LORD, AND NEVER WILL.

Then he began coughing and wincing in pain and put his hand on his lower abdomen—which had been hurting more and more of late.

Minutes later, after coughing up a few drops of blood, he laid the gun down and got himself a glass of water. He took two pills from a small container in his pocket, washed them down his throat, and looked at himself in a mirror.

Feeling slightly better, he placed the shotgun back in the cabinet and locked it.

He went out on his porch, looked up, and noticed a big flock of Canada geese honking and flying in formation over Watauga Lake. Far below them he could make out a group of young men and women canoeing and merrily splashing themselves with their paddles—as if they didn't have a worry in the world.

I might be living in a troubled world but nature is always perfect, he thought, *and oh, to be young and wild and free again.*

CHAPTER 19

Memorable Day

At the altar, staring dreamily into each other's eyes, William and Leigh said their vows. They had memorized them, and so with Reverend Hicks standing between them and holding a Bible, the short, but meaningful, ceremony went smoothly.

Next to them were Raymond, William's best man, and Gwen, a bridesmaid. Sitting in the front row in one of the little church's old pine hewn pews were Ed and Madge, and Ann and Ted. Seated right behind them were John and Doc and others.

The sanctuary, decorated with flowers and cuttings from trees, was packed with friends from Laketon, students from the university and other well-wishers.

"I now pronounce you man and wife," Reverend Hicks said with a smile. "You may kiss the bride, William."

The groom took Leigh in his arms and gave her a long, lingering kiss.

So long that people in the church began to wonder when he'd let her breathe.

"He can flat out let her go now," one onlooker said to her husband. "Ain't no need squeezin' and suckin' the life outta' her the first day they're married."

"I'd say she's used ta it," said the man, not taking his eyes off the stirring scene at the altar. "Why, I 'member when you an' me used ta have quite a time out by the barn."

"Shut your mouth, you fool," she chided him. "You're in God's house."

William finally removed his mouth from Leigh's lips and his arms from around her waist.

Reverend Hicks looked out at those seated in the pews and announced: "Ladies and gentlemen, I give you Mr. and Mrs. William Edward Anderson."

Clapping, hollering and whistling ensued as the young happy couple walked down the aisle.

They didn't notice Buzz, a sinister smirk on his face, sitting in the last pew.

They navigated the front steps of the church carefully, with William helping Leigh gather her long wedding dress so that she wouldn't trip. Outside in the courtyard, they were showered with buttercups, red and white roses, and festive confetti.

As the church slowly emptied, Ed noticed Buzz but ignored him, making his way out onto the grounds.

No way I'm gonna let that scoundrel ruin my day, Ed thought.

"Hey Big Brother!" Buzz shouted.

Ed turned around, faced him and said, "I told you what would happen if you ever came back here."

"My goodness, Ed. Is that anyway to greet your only brother?"

"YOU ARE NOT MY BROTHER," Ed said, trying to control his anger.

But that strident pronouncement seemed to roll off Buzz like water off a duck's back.

"Surely, you wouldn't want me to miss my own daughter's wedding," he declared.

"What do you want, Buzz?"

Looking around to make sure no one could hear them, Buzz said, "I want a hundred thousand dollars in cash. As in God We Trust. And if you think you can just kill me and your troubles'll be over, you better think again.

"Because if any harm comes to me, I have William's x-rays that I happened to come across in your friend's clinic last night."

"So, you broke into Doc Anderson's office?! You will pay for what you are doing, as God is my witness," Ed declared.

Seemingly ignoring that utterance, Buzz continued, "And, so as I was sayin', if anything bad happens to me, those x-rays'll be discovered, and goat boy's life will never be the same.

"Now listen up," Buzz added. "Where the A.T. crosses the highway by the lake, there's a pull off. Be there at 2 p.m. tomorrow. I'll pull off and you'll hand me the money in a small travel bag. And that's the last time I promise you'll ever see me.

"And if you're not there with the money, goat boy will be the biggest news of the year. Wonder what those bloodsucking newscasters would say about your goat boy?"

Buzz began to walk away, but not before bidding Ed farewell and saying he looked forward to meeting up with him tomorrow afternoon.

"You better be there, Big Brother, because if you ain't, your life and the life of your son'll be a living misery."

*****

As Ed wondered about where or how he'd be able to come up with so much cash, he noticed Doc talking to a police officer. It was apparently something important because the officer was taking notes and peppering Doc with questions.

"I need to leave, Ed," Doc said a few seconds later. "Someone noticed the back door of the clinic ajar and called the cops. Seems someone broke in last night. Most likely a drug addict."

Ed said, "It was Buzz. He's demanding more money. He's got William's x-rays."

"Oh my Lord! I knew I shoulda installed an alarm system years ago. Damn!"

Ed said the break-in was in no way his fault.

"Stick with probably a drug addict, Doc, till I figure out what to do. I'll call you tonight."

*****

After they'd changed into clothes for traveling, the newly married young couple piled into a late model sedan Ted had given them as a wedding gift. It had been decorated by friends, with "JUST MARRIED" written on the back window and a string of cans tied to the rear bumper.

"Have a wonderful trip!" Ed yelled to them.

"Thank you, Dad!" said Leigh, who had lately begun referring to him like that. "I'll take good care of your boy!"

Ed bent down, leaned into the car, and took his son by the shoulders. "You're a man now and I want you to know how proud I am of you. And you know how glad I am that you came into my life?"

Ed began choking up.

William, hugging him, said, "You know I'm coming back, Dad. I love you. I'll give you a call in three or four days."

Everyone cheered as Madge and Ed, tears in their eyes, watched the car pull off.

"I can't believe they're all grown up and gone, now," Ed said. "Seems like only yesterday he was a newborn in the barn. And Leigh, the way she came into this world, was hard to say the least. And now look at 'her! Ain't she the cutest little wife you ever saw?"

Madge wrapped her arms tightly around him and said she had her toothbrush with her.

CHAPTER 20

Dead Reckoning

The day after the wedding, sunny with a light breeze, Ed sat at a table in the kitchen writing a letter.

"Dear Madge: By the time you read this my troubles with Buzz will be over and I'll no longer be in pain. Buzz was blackmailing me, and my time was limited. Doc can explain everything.

"I'm sorry it had to end like this, but I saw no other way. William knows nothing of this, so it is up to you if you want to divulge anything. Or I was simply driving too fast. I love you more than anything and I have been truly blessed to have you in my life. Ed."

He signed the letter, put it in an envelope, wrote Madge on the outside of it, and laid it on the table.

A small travel bag was on the table, and sad-eyed, droopy-eared Winston lay nearby.

Ed nervously watched the kitchen clock. It was 1:47.

He winced in pain and leaned forward, dropping his head.

The phone on the kitchen wall rang and he answered it.

"I got it, Ed," said Doc, in Buzz's motel room holding the large manila envelope with William's name on it.

"Thank God. Did you have any trouble getting in?"

Doc said, "Would you believe the housekeeper was cleaning the room and I looked in. And she said she'd be out of here in one minute and she was."

"Where was the envelope?"

"Under the mattress," Doc snickered. "Buzz didn't have much of an imagination when it came to hiding things."

"Thank you, Doc., and thanks for helping me keep William safe all these years. You're a true friend. I love you, man."

"Ed, Ed, hello?"

But Ed had hung up the phone and now was nervously watching the kitchen clock again. It was 1:50. He picked up the travel bag, fought the urge to vomit, and patted Winston's head.

"So long, Winston. You take care of Madge for me."

He and the dog, looking forlorn, walked out the back door, and Winston watched and whined as Ed got in his truck and pulled out.

He drove a short distance, then pulled off near the sign for the Appalachian Trail, a picture of a hiker with the letter 'A.T.' at the top.

Turning off the ignition, Ed—again fighting pain—bent over, took a bottle of pills out of his shirt pocket and swallowed several.

About a minute later, Buzz drove up in his yellow Cadillac convertible, with the top up.

Ed, carrying the travel bag, got out of his pickup and approached Buzz's car.

His stepbrother gave him a thumbs up, rolled down the window and said, "Open it."

"Are you sure, Buzz?"

"I didn't come all the way out here just for the scenery!" he snapped. "Now open that damn bag!"

"Time is money as they always say," Ed said coolly and calmly as he unzipped the bag, pulled out a 38-

calibre Smith and Wesson revolver, and aimed it at Buzz.

"Now move your butt over," Ed commanded him.

When Buzz refused, Ed jammed the gun into Buzz's crotch and threatened to make him a girl.

"Or if you don't want to be a girl, you'll end up a eunuch!"

Buzz, beads of sweat on his forehead, slid over while Ed got behind the wheel and pulled out fast, burning rubber in the Cadillac.

"What're you wantin'? Where we goin'?"

When Ed didn't answer, Buzz reminded him that if anything happened to him, William would be exposed. "And be careful with my car, Ed. It' a classic."

Tires squealed as they rounded a curve on the two-lane, winding mountain highway.

"What year did you say this Cadillac was," Ed asked.

"It's a 1955 El Dorado. Now slow down!"

"You shoulda' got a later model—one with airbags. Better fasten your seatbelt, Buzz."

"That ain't funny, Ed. Now where the hell are we goin'?"

Ed smiled and said, "Just for a little drive around the lake. I ain't never driven a Cadillac."

They were going 70 miles per hour, according to the speedometer. Tires squealed as they rounded another curve—rocky cliffs overgrown with kudzu on one side of the road and a steep embankment leading down to the lake on the other side.

"My God, Ed! Slow down before you kill us both!"

"It doesn't matter, Buzz. I don't have long to live anyway."

"Well, I'm sorry, Big Brother, but I do."

Ed grinned, gripped the steering wheel more firmly, and asked him if he was sure about that.

"You better think about William, Ed. What'll his life be like if somethin' happens to me and the x-rays get discovered? You forgettin' about that?"

Then Buzz grabbed the bag and unzipped it. It was stuffed with magazines.

"Where's the damn money?" he demanded. "I told you what would happen if you didn't do what I said. Now for sure I'm takin' William's x-rays to the Johnson City Press."

"I'm not worryin' about that anymore, Buzz. You see, Doc has the x-rays."

"You're a lyin' son-of-a-bitch!"

"Nope. It's the truth, Buzz. Doc got 'em from under your mattress at the Riverview Motel. Just like you to be so careless about where you stashed 'em."

Shocked and desperate, Buzz grabbed the gun that Ed had laid on the seat between them. He pointed it at Ed.

"Stop this damn car right now or I swear I'll blow your brains out!"

"There's no bullets in it, Buzz," said Ed, pressing his foot even more forcefully on the gas pedal.

Buzz pulled the trigger again and again, then tried to hit Ed with the pistol. But Ed blocked the blows with his hand, snatched the gun from him, and tossed it out the window.

Tires squealed at every turn as the speedometer now read 75.

"Okay, Okay! You win! Just slow down! Let me out! You can even keep the damn car."

"No thanks, Buzz. This is too much car for me to handle. And where I'm goin', I'll never need it."

"Okay, then. Just let me out. I swear to God, you'll never see me again. I'm beggin' you, Ed. You don't need to do this."

"Oh, but I do. You'd never stop, Buzz. You took money from me, your own stepbrother, and you'd do it again and again—every time you needed more. And after I was gone, you'd take money from William and Leigh, your own daughter.

"And by the way, Buzz, the only good thing to come out of your life is Leigh. She happens to be a wonderful young lady, as is her mom, Ann, who you almost beat to death."

"I would never take anything from Leigh," he said.

"Sure you would, Buzz. For a long time I could never understand how you could hurt people like you do. People that love you or try to love you. Then it finally dawned on me. Some people are just plain evil. And nothing anyone can do will ever change that."

Buzz stared at Ed expressionless. He flinched every time the tires squealed, and now they were squealing more often as the car increased in speed and often crossed the center median line, veering dangerously into the other lane.

"You feel you can get away with anything so that's what you do," Ed said.

"Quit preachin' to me, Big Brother!"

"If I were you, Buzz, I'd be sayin' my prayers. And if you don't listen ta me, I'll just kill us both right now."

"Okay. Say your piece, BUT SLOW DOWN!"

"As I was about ta say, stealin' from family is no problem for you, Buzz. You're incapable of loving anyone but yourself. And I know you think I hate you, but I actually feel sorry for you.

"But having said that," Ed added, "I refuse to let you destroy the lives of people I love. Good people. Caring, honest people. So this world'll be better off without you, Buzz."

The car's speedometer now read 100.

"For God's sake, Ed, stop this craziness! I'm your brother!"

"Stepbrother," Ed corrected him for the umpteenth time.

The Cadillac, now topping 100 miles per hour, sped down a long downhill straight stretch of highway with the Butler Bridge, spanning a 300-ft. deep section of Watauga Lake, at the bottom of a hill.

A long gravel parallel pull-off was to the left of the highway with a guardrail running perpendicular to the road at the end. On the other side of the guardrail was a 40-ft. drop to the cold blue waters of the lake.

The Cadillac sped toward the pull-off heading for the guardrail to the left of the bridge.

Buzz screamed, "I can't swim, Ed!"

"It doesn't matter," said Ed as the car crashed against the guard rail, taking part of the corrugated steel structure with it on its long flight, like a missile, to the lake.

The car created a huge splash, bobbed, and made a gurgling sound for a few seconds, then sank out of sight.

In the dense, dark woods near the bridge, a momma bear and her two cubs watched the crash and then went about their business scrounging for food.

CHAPTER 21

The Lord Has His Reason

On a sunny, cloudless day at the family cemetery, a plain pine casket was lowered into the ground.

Gathered on one side of the burial site were those who had been closest to Ed—William, Madge, Leigh, Doc, Raymond, and John. And of course, his beloved dog Winston.

On the other end were Ann, Ted, Gwen, and longtime friends and neighbors of Ed—going back to his days growing up in Laketon.

Reverend Hicks, wearing a clerical collar and dark blue suit, gave the simple, but profound eulogy.

It ended with, "Lord, Ed Anderson was truly a good man, and we were all blessed to have known him."

(6 Years Later)

A late model SUV pulls up to a modern one-story building with a sign out front that says, "ORTHOPEDIC SOLUTIONS."

Inside the front of the vehicle on this sunny, winter day is an older Leigh, driving, and older William in the passenger seat.

"Did you call Madge and tell her we'd be there Wednesday afternoon?" William asked.

Leigh said she had, and that John, Raymond, Gwen, and Doc were also coming for Thanksgiving dinner.

"What about me, too? I'll be there," said their son, little Eddie, riding in the back in a car seat.

"For heaven's sakes, we almost forgot about Eddie, Mom," William said.

The little boy giggled, and William kissed his wife.

"Thanks for lunch, sweetheart," he said. "See ya later tonight, and you, too, Eddie."

Eddie waved at his dad as he got out of the car and entered the modern brick medical building.

"I'm back, Sharon," William said as he walked past the reception desk.

"Okay, Dr. Anderson. I put the Smiths with Tucker in room 2."

William walked down a hall, with paintings of wildlife and Watauga Lake on each side of the wall, and entered an office with a glass door that read "William E. Anderson, M.D." He then hung his heavy winter coat on a hook in a closet near the door and slipped into a white jacket with "Dr. Anderson" embroidered above the left breast pocket.

Room 2 down the hall was where Mr. and Mrs. Smith, along with their 6-year-old son Tucker, were waiting for him. It was a large space with an examining table, a stool, a cabinet with medical supplies, and several chairs. One wall featured a large color portrait of a man in a Tennessee Titans uniform holding a football. It was signed: Raymond Washington

The well-dressed but anxious-looking couple rose to introduce themselves when William entered the room.

"We've heard a lot about you, Dr. Anderson," Mrs. Smith said. "And we thank you for taking our son Tucker as a patient.

The cute little boy, in his dad's lap, had blond hair with bangs hanging down over the tops of his blue eyes. He was playing with a toy firetruck.

"Mr. Smith, I'm William Anderson, and this must be Tucker. Let's put Tucker here, so I can get a good look at him."

The father, also thanking William for seeing their boy, placed his son on a small, padded examining table.

William, with his stethoscope, listened to Tucker's heart for about 30 seconds. Then he sat down on the stool and moved closer to the little boy. He took Tucker's leg and felt all around his stump.

"So, Tucker, are you in school yet?"

"Yes sir. I'm in the first grade. I couldn't go last year cause a my leg. And my friends call me Tuck."

"Then I'll call you Tuck. Because I want to be one of your friends."

Tuck laughed and said, "Okay."

"Does this hurt when I push here?"

"Nope."

"How about here?"

"Nope."

William felt for movement in the stump as he asked Tuck a few questions about what he liked to do.

"Now close your eyes and pretend like you still have your foot and point your big toe at your nose, Tuck."

Tucker, chuckling, said, "I pointed my big toe at you, Dad."

William stood up. "Very good, Tuck. You know what? I think we can make you just like new."

"Will I be able to walk again?"

"You'll be able to walk good" said William, as he paced back and forth across the room. "And run good," said William, as he ran in place. "And even dance good." William did a little dance.

"As good as you?" Tuck asked.

"I don't see why not. It'll take some practice, but you'll be able to do it."

William then reached down and pulled both of his own pant legs up, revealing two artificial lower legs made of titanium. They extended down into his white leather shoes.

Tucker's eyes got big and excited, and he opened his mouth wide.

His mom cried tears of joy while his dad cracked a huge smile.

As William bid the Smiths farewell and returned to his office, his thoughts turned to long ago:

Dad, why did God want me to have special feet anyway?

I'm not sure, son, but I am sure he had a good reason.

*****

A few days later, the Anderson family and their close friends—Madge, William, Leigh, Eddie in a highchair, Raymond, Gwen, John, and Doc—met for a Thanksgiving feast at Ed's homeplace.

They bowed their heads as Raymond began saying the blessing.

Everyone laughed and William and Raymond tapped their glasses together when Raymond spoke about the food they were about to "tackle."

During their laughter, William gave Winston two bites of turkey.

Meanwhile, the little wooden man danced outside while heavy, wet snow transformed the farm into a winter wonderland.

Just maybe, with a little help from Ed.

BIO for Larry Timbs Jr.

Larry Timbs Jr. is a Vietnam-era U.S. Air Force veteran, a former professional journalist and a retired university professor.

A native of the mountains of East Tennessee, he currently lives with his wife Patsy about three miles from the ocean in Surfside Beach, South Carolina.

He's a freelance writer for the Charleston (South Carolina) Post and Courier and for MyHorryNews.com

Timbs loves dogs and he has a strong interest in the supernatural.

His previous books are *Fish Springs: Beneath the Surface* (2014), with Michael Manuel; *Justice for Toby* (2016) with Michael Manuel; *Unlikeliest Witness: An Appalachian Story of Suspense* (2018); *From the Beak of An Eagle: Memoirs of a Winthrop Faculty Member* (2021); and *Harmless News in Myrtle Beach: A Journalist Seeks the Truth About UFOs* (2022).

He can be reached at: larrytimbs@gmail.com

BIO for Michael Manual

Michael Manuel finished high school on the Mississippi Gulf Coast and attended The University of Southern Mississippi. He and his wife Joyce live on a mountain, overlooking Watauga Lake near Hampton, Tennessee.

They are active in the First United Methodist church in Elizabethton, Tennessee, and Michael is also an active member of the Carter County Car Club.

They like to hike on the Appalachian Trail, just below the house and kayak on the lake. The Manuels each have a daughter.

Michael co-authored two other books with Larry Timbs Jr.—*Fish Springs: Beneath the Surface* and *Justice for Toby*.

Michael's last published book was *The Last Fishing Trip*.

He is also a screen writer and has written screen plays for all four books.

His email address is:

bearhavenproductions@gmail.com

Made in the USA
Middletown, DE
12 January 2025